RAMBLING DOWN THE RANGE

A COLLECTION OF WESTERN SHORT STORIES

RAMBLING DOWN THE RANGE

A COLLECTION OF
WESTERN SHORT STORIES

DUSTY RICHARDS

THREE-TIME SPUR AWARD WINNER

HAT CREEK

HAT CREEK

an imprint of
Roan & Weatherford Publishing Associates, LLC
Bentonville, Arkansas • Heber City, Utah
www.roanweatherford.com

Library of Congress Cataloging-in-Publication Data
Names: Richards, Dusty., author
Title: Rambling Down the Range/Dusty Richards
Description: First Edition | Bentonville: Hat Creek, 2025.
Identifiers: LCCN: 2025947795 | IBSN: 979-8-89299-093-6 (hardcover) |
979-8-89299-094-3 (trade paperback) | ISBN: 979-8-89299-095-0 (eBook)
Subjects: FICTION/Westerns | FICTION/Short Stories (single author) |
FICTION/Historical/General
LC record available at: https://lccn.loc.gov.2025947795

Hat Creek paperback edition December, 2025

Cover Design by Casey W. Cowan
Interior Design by John Bredesen
Editing by Dennis Doty & Don Money

This book is a work of historical fiction. Apart from the well-known actual people, events, and locales that figure in the narrative, all names, characters, places, and incidents are the product of the author's imagination or are used fictitiously. Any resemblance to current events or locales, or to living persons, is entirely coincidental.

This book is dedicated to all the many members of the Northwest Arkansas Writers Workshop, including Velda Brotherton, Linda Apple, Mike Miller, Lisa Wingate, Casey Cowan, Pamela Foster, Ruth Weeks, Greg Camp, Richard Howk, Gil Miller, James Newman, Patty Stith, Lori Ericson, Jan Morrill, Douglas Jones, Peter Jeppsen, Vivian Cummings, Duke Pennell, Julie James, and many, many more.

CONTENTS

AUTHOR'S NOTE

HERE IS MY NEW COLLECTION of yarns seeped in alkali dust, fresh piney aromas, creosote brush, spiny cactus, and with low flying, disinterested in the living buzzards. It is about the men and women who hammered out the land Jefferson bought, and the rest added to west of the Mississippi River to form this great nation of ours.

Throughout my career I have written lots of western short stories. In fact, my earliest effort was two short stories that changed my life. I was in Missouri in February 1985, at a writer's conference at Branson and met a very prolific western writer, Jory Sherman. When I told him I had sold two western stories, he said I could belong to WWA. I knew that wouldn't get me into that prestigious group of writers, but he insisted, and I went home, filled out the application, and with a check for say fifty dollars mailed it to them. I was wrong. They accepted me with open arms and open hearts.

My wife, Pat, and I drove to San Antonio through a ten-inch deluge of rain that June, and I got to meet the gods of the Western Word. I'd read them all. I learned so damn much at that convention my head swelled two sizes. I went home full of dreams of how my pile of books would soon be tucked under breathtaking covers and on every rack in every store with my fellow Western writers.

Back at the next regional writers' conference in Branson, Missouri I also met a man, Dr. Frank Reuter, who edited big name authors in New York. I sent him one of my best. It came back bloodier with red ink than a Civil War battle. I edited it like he said, then wrote a new one and sent it to him. It had whole pages he never wrote on. Book three, he edited it, and I drove over to his house for all the oral help I could pry out of him.

The conversation went like this.

> "How did it go, Frank?"
> "I probably didn't edit it as hard as I did the others."
> "Why not?"
> "I was so busy reading your damn story."

Here was a man who edited big-time bestsellers for a living. If my old cowboy book had him wanting to read it, I had a winner. I sold *Noble's Way* a few years later.

A few years after that sale, the late Peggy Fielding came by my house to spend the night and asked if I didn't have a lot of short stories. When I said yes, she asked why I hadn't I published them?

"'Cause I ain't Louis L'Amour. He's the only one who could sell any short stories like that."

She collared Dan Case, a small publisher from Denton, Texas. He offered me a contract, then called me on the phone and asked me on the phone what we should call the book.

I chose *Waltzing with Tumbleweeds.* The title simply came from off the top of my head and worked. For the cover, he used a photo of a famous writer and friend, Chuck Sasser, roping on his best horse. Call it fate, his poor horse died of colic twenty-four hours later. The collection was out for years, and one weekend we gave the E version away free. Ten thousand copies went out. Over the next eighteen months, we sold almost twenty-thousand more. Not bad for an old cowboy.

The title of that first short story collection gave us the idea for this one. *Rambling Down the Range* seemed to be the perfect companion to *Waltz-*

ing with Tumbleweeds, evoking that same sense of restless, gritty, cowboy wanderlust that attracted me to the cowboy life in the first place. If you've never stood at the foot of the Front Range of the Rockies, looking up in wonder at those massive, snow-capped peaks, you're missing one of the most awe-inspiring sites in the world.

I'd like to give a special thanks to Casey Cowan, the one-man machine who keeps Roan & Weatherford Publishing going, and especially the Hat Creek Division, which does Westerns, and *Saddlebag Dispatches,* the western magazine we founded together in 2014. Many thanks also to George "Clay" Mitchell, chief developmental editor of the outfit, for helping whip my stories into shape; Amy Cowan, who not only chases down the commas and the typos like Sherlock Holmes did crime, but wrangles all the numbers on the back end, as well; and Dennis Doty, the curmudgeonly retired rodeo cowboy and Marine NCO who runs *Saddlebag Dispatches.* Last but not least, thanks to that entire crew of helpers who keep the wagon wheels under and our operation rolling.

May the Good Lord bless and keep *mis amigos.*
Dusty Richards

FOREWORD

WHEN PEOPLE TALK ABOUT THE great chroniclers of the American West, certain names rise to the top again and again—Louis L'Amour, Zane Grey, Elmer Kelton, Larry McMurtry. Each in his own way helped shape how generations of readers imagine the frontier: the sweep of the land, the hardships of survival, the bonds of loyalty and love that defined a people. To that list, without hesitation, I add the name Dusty Richards. Not just because of his astonishing output—over 150 published novels and countless short stories—but because of the authenticity, heart, and sheer humanity that he poured into every line. Dusty didn't just write Westerns. He lived them, breathed them, and taught the rest of us why they still matter.

Dusty's achievements speak for themselves. Three Spur Awards from the Western Writers of America. Multiple Will Rogers Medallion Awards. A Western Heritage Wrangler Award. The kind of accolades that confirm what his readers always knew: he was one of the best. But what those plaques and trophies can't capture is his relentless drive to keep writing, keep learning, and keep stretching himself. He never wrote the same story twice. He was always looking for new characters, new corners of the frontier, new ways to tell the story of America through the lens of the West.

That's part of what makes *Rambling Down the Range* so special. These are stories from Dusty's later career, pieces that reveal not just his craftsmanship, but also his willingness to take risks and follow his heart. Many of them lean into romance. Not in the formulaic sense, but in the truest meaning of the word. Romance of the land, romance of human connection, romance of the possibilities that drew people westward in the first place. Dusty understood that the frontier wasn't only about gunfights and cattle drives. It was also about longing, about hope, about the need for love and belonging in a world that could be cold and unforgiving.

Some of these stories first appeared in the pages of *Saddlebag Dispatches*, a magazine Dusty and I co-founded with the dream of giving Western writers a vibrant home in the twenty-first century. Others remained unpublished, set aside during his lifetime, now brought together at last. Taken as a whole, they remind us that Dusty never stopped exploring the range— geographically, historically, emotionally. He could move from the biting chill of a Dakota winter to the dusty heat of an Arizona arroyo with ease. He could give us hardened outlaws and tender lovers in the same breath. That balance—between toughness and tenderness—is part of what made him truly unique.

Longtime readers will recognize Dusty's hallmarks here. His eye for detail, his ear for authentic dialogue, his deep knowledge of Western history and culture. But they may also find themselves surprised by the depth of emotion, the quieter moments, the glimpses into the inner lives of characters who might in another writer's hands have remained stock figures. Dusty believed in the humanity of the West—in its women as much as its men, in its Mexican vaqueros and Native warriors as much as its Anglo cowhands. He sought to write the West as it truly was, diverse, complex, and full of voices worth hearing.

For me, personally, editing and publishing these stories is more than a professional responsibility. It's a way of keeping Dusty's voice alive, of carrying forward the work we started together. His passing in 2018 left a hole in my life and in the Western community, but it didn't silence him. Every time I return to his stories, I hear him again, telling tales, cracking jokes, spinning yarns, challenging me to think bigger about what the Western can be. That's the mark of a true storyteller. Even when he's gone, he keeps talking to us through the words he left behind.

Readers sometimes ask me what makes a Dusty Richards story different. My answer is simple. Dusty wrote with heart. He understood that the West was never just a backdrop of mountains and mesas. It was a stage where people wrestled with timeless questions—justice, loyalty, survival, faith, love. That's why his stories still resonate. They aren't relics. They're alive, full of the same struggles and hopes we carry today.

So, whether this is your first time picking up Dusty Richards or you've been riding alongside him for decades, I invite you to settle in with Rambling Down the Range. Let Dusty take you where he always loved to go, down the trails and canyons, across the rivers and ridges, into the hearts of men and women who embody the spirit of the American West. These are not just stories. They're reminders of who we are, where we came from, and what endures.

For Dusty, the range never ended. And thanks to collections like this one, it never will.

Casey W. Cowan
President & CEO, Oghma Communications
Co-Founder, *Saddlebag Dispatches* Magazine
Bentonville, Arkansas
September 9, 2025

RAMBLING DOWN THE RANGE

A COLLECTION OF
WESTERN SHORT STORIES

MINDING HIS BUSINESS

J EB SIMMS WAS MINDING HIS own business when he reined his dun
horse down the cow trail that led to the Verde River. He rode him under
some ancient gnarled-trunk cottonwoods rattling leaves over his head in
the afternoon breeze to look at the running water of the stream. Dismounted,
his pony dropped his head down to graze on the short grass on the sandy flood
plain. He wouldn't go nowhere.

Why, he had this whole place to himself and the ravens. He put his gun
belt on the horn of the saddle first, then his weather-beaten felt hat. Sitting
on the sandy ground, he twisted off his boots, socks, then shed his pants,
vest, and shirt. In his long handles, with a bar of soap and a towel he went
down to the water. In a hole that looked deeper than the rest of the stream, he
waded in. He seated himself neck deep and soaked, then he began scrubbing
his underwear. He had soon washed the underwear where he could reach it,
then he shed it, soaped the rest, then sloshed it around to get the soap off.

The sun felt warm after he got over the first chill the evaporation gave
him getting out, and he laid the one piece to dry on the taller grass. He did the

same with the long-sleeved shirt and jeans. It all took some time, but he had lots of that. Sitting chest deep in the swirling stream, he soaped his body and the hair on his head. He sure felt relaxed watching a buzzard or two drift by.

Kind of nice to have the world to himself, no big pressing deals or things on his mind. He dried off and put on his near dried underwear. The shirt and jeans needed more time to dry.

He heard a horse snorting sound and then saw it, weary-like, coming off the slope from the east. Was there a rider coming? He pulled on his jeans, stuck his hat on, and about had his gun belt buckled on when he saw someone looking passed out in the saddle coming down the far slope on that horse. Her hands appeared to be tied to the saddle horn. He rushed across the stream to see about the two.

"Whoa." He caught the numb acting horse by the bridle headstall. The reins had been broken. He shook the young woman in the saddle by the arm to wake her.

"Huh?" She jerked her head up and blinked her eyes at him. "Who are you?"

"Jeb Simms." He went to untying her hands. "Who did this to you?"

She fainted, and he caught her in his arms. Finally, with the sharp knife from his belt holster, he sliced the rope, freed her hands, and took her off the saddle. The horse, anxious to cure his thirst, shuffled on down and drank water. Jeb carefully laid her on the grass.

"Lady, you need to come to. I am no doctor. Now, who tied you to that horn, and where are they at?" He was closely watching the east side for anyone pursuing her.

"They kidnapped me."

"Well, who were they, and why did they do that?"

"Spurlock and Nacho."

"Don't know them. You aren't in too good a shape."

"They drugged me so—"

He was on his knees and about beside himself to do something to help her. What if those kidnappers came and caught him? They damn sure might shoot him and her too. How would he ever get her to his place?

There was nowhere else to go with her—close by.

His headquarters was three miles up the river bottoms and on a mountainside bench above that. He carried her across the knee-deep river in his arms, and halfway across, almost tripped and spilled her in the water. On the far side, he found a place to lay her on the ground. Fetching his canteen, he gave her some water. He made her sip it slow.

When he figured she had enough, she pushed it away and closed her eyes. Damn, what could he do with her? Take her to his place and try to save her. When did she eat last? No telling. But she was weak.

He finished dressing. Then he located some poles and his old belt to strap them to his own saddle horn. Next, he used his lariat to make a holder for her across the poles and a small blanket on top of the web work. He'd fashioned a travois and loaded the limp passed out girl on it. Still watching for the kidnappers, he hoped she didn't die on him because he didn't even know her name.

He wanted her horse to come along. But without reins, he would be hard to lead. The weary acting horse came along with him like he was lonesome. He made his own mount walk slow. Every time one of those poles went over a rock and fell, it gave her a hard jolt.

How old was she? He didn't know. She wasn't a child or a very old woman.

At last, he came up to his log house and carried her inside. She was sleeping and breathing all right. She'd wake up some time. After placing her on his bed, he went outside and unsaddled the two horses to turn them loose in the corral. Her horse had a shoulder brand, 7K. He'd never heard of that outfit.

No sign of any pursuit by her kidnappers. Back in the house, he built a fire in the wood-burning stove to cook them some supper. Maybe he'd fix oatmeal because he could make that quicker. She moaned, and he went to see about her lying on his bed.

"Who are you?" she asked groggily.

"Jeb Simms. Same guy that found you. I brought you up here. You fainted."

"I—I don't know you."

"I was taking a bath when you showed up with your hands tied to the saddle horn, and the reins were broken. Your bay horse is in the corral."

"He isn't my horse. I am Cal Rhodes's daughter. You know him?"

He'd heard of him. "He owns a big ranch up north of here. We never met. How did you get way down here?"

"Two men kidnapped me three days ago. I think that long ago. They kept me doped and demanded a ten-thousand-dollar ransom. Dad's men must have tracked them down, but they botched saving me, and those two ran like hell and took me along. I broke away from them, but I could not rein my horse with my hands tied to the horn. I lost consciousness."

"What can I do for you?" he asked, seeing she was in a frantic way.

"Let me go outside."

"Go. It is around the far side."

She hurried outside and came back real weak looking. Barely able to get inside the door, he told her to get back on the bed.

Wooden-like, she obeyed.

"I have some oatmeal. Can you sit up and eat some? I can feed it to you."

"Would you?"

He helped her sit up, propped by the pillows.

She ate really slow and about went to sleep doing that. After he had half a bowl of cereal in her, she waved the next spoon away. "'Nough." She snuggled down and went to sleep.

He ate the rest of the oatmeal he'd made and covered her with a blanket. At that point, it was dark. She was not that big all covered up. Seated he took off his boots and gun belt and took the south half of the bed to sleep on. She wasn't using that part of the mattress anyway.

He woke up in the night. She was slamming him with a pillow. He guessed for lack of something better and shouting, "You no good son of a bitch. You have ruined my reputation. What do you mean by sleeping with me?"

Finally, he took the pillow away from her and caught her wrists. "Settle down little lady. I have not done one thing to you but save you, feed you, and let you share my bed. Now, calm down. We both have been fully dressed and asleep until you went crazy."

"What do you intend to do with me?"

"Well, Miss Haughty, I was going to take you back home today. I figure it will take three days to get you back there. But you were so tired last night, I wasn't sure you'd make the trip back starting today."

"My father will repay you."

"I'm not looking for any pay. If I had a daughter, and she wandered off or was kidnapped, I'd want her back home too."

"I didn't wander off as you say away from home. I was kidnapped."

"Fine. I need to catch another horse to pack our bedroll and supplies."

"I am not sleeping with you tonight or any night on any bedroll."

"Fine. You can wrap up in a blanket. Lady, I have no desire to abuse you. Sooner I get you home, sooner I'll be back here enjoying the peace and quiet of my life.

"Hmmm."

"I'll fry us some taters and bacon. That suit you for breakfast?"

"Fine. So, then we can get moving and get me back home."

"That suits me fine."

"I think you tried to take advantage of me sleeping beside me."

"I never touched you."

"I am not so sure."

"Well, you are in one piece, looks like to me."

It was cracking daylight. She got up and went outside to use the facilities. He made coffee and hashed up two large potatoes in the hot bacon grease. She finally came back in and peered in his skillet.

"Why, you didn't even peel them."

"I washed them. That skin won't kill you."

"I never saw that done before. I would have peeled them. You have a hairbrush I can use?"

"Over on the dresser."

She nodded and found it. Armed with his brush she worked for the next ten minutes pulling out the tangles and wincing while she brushed her shoulder-length brown hair. He poured her a cup of coffee, and she looked around cleaning all the hair she'd lost out of the brush. She looked around for someplace to trash it. In the end, she got up and threw it out the door.

"I don't have a cow or any sugar. I live simple. I drink it black. Sorry."

"Never tried it like that."

"First time for everything."

"I never thought of it like that. There really is."

"Now, I wonder how come you are dressed like a boy?"

"I was riding a new horse when they kidnapped me. I always dress like this when I ride horses back up on the ranch. No one but the cowboys see me. I am my father's tomboy, I guess. But I am glad they didn't kidnap me in a dress."

"I bet so."

He dished her out the bacon-potato hash on a plate she had inspected earlier. Like it might be unwashed or something, and she was being damn certain about it. But she must have liked the coffee. She drank half of it. She tried to straighten the bent fork but gave up and went to eating with it.

"This is not bad," she said between bites.

"It will fill your insides."

"I usually have eggs, bacon, and bread for my breakfast or pancakes with syrup. I could drink your coffee without sugar and cream. It is very good."

"Arbuckle. I am not a tea man, and I was raised on scorched barley coffee 'cause we could not afford anything else."

She made a face. "Oh, I had some of that at a neighbor's house once. It is terrible tasting, even with cream and sugar."

"When that is all you have, you eat it or drink it," he said between bites.

"Where were you raised?"

"East Texas, on a sharecropper's cotton patch."

"Did you go to school?"

"I can read and write and do math. We had some three-month classes each winter. The rest of the time we farmed forty acres. Cotton is a thirteen month a year crop."

She made a sour face. "Pardon but there are only twelve months in a year."

"No, ma'am. On a cotton farm, there are thirteen. You can't get it all done in twelve."

At that point she laughed. "I don't see any cotton growing up here."

"Right. That's why I live up here, little lady."

She swept her light brown hair back from her face. "My name is not Little Lady. My name is Veronica Rhodes."

"Well, I thought that was a secret you used, so I won't know your true identity."

She frowned at him and then went back to eating. Obviously, she was hungry, and the potato skins weren't holding her back. "'My mother left the ranch,' they said, when I was three. I don't recall her. We have a photograph of her when my father first met her in Fort Worth. She never wrote either one of us a letter. I don't know if she's alive or dead. Dad says he never got a notice of her divorcing him, but she may have married someone else, and who knows?"

"She must have had strong reasons to turn her back on you at that age?"

"Or she didn't give a damn, right?"

"I bet you thought that early on."

She dropped her head and nodded.

"Your dad is a big successful rancher from all I've heard. He never had her looked for by a lawyer or a detective back there?"

"He said he did, when I was little, and they found no sign of her."

"He never remarried?"

"He said, 'Once burned, never again.'"

"So, you are his treasure?"

"I guess so."

"Well, if we keep riding, we should be there in two or three days."

"I can wash these dishes while you saddle up."

"We'll need them packed in our gear. That bent fork is the best one of two I have, Veronica."

"I will wash them and the tin cups when we finish the pot."

"It goes too."

"I'll get it all."

"I'm sorry—"

"Heavens, Jeb Simms, you don't have to apologize to me. You saved me from many things including being dead somewhere if you hadn't taken the trouble to save me. I owe you my life, sir."

"Just Jeb from the Texas cotton patch, ma'am."

"Times I want to beat on you with the sides of my fists."

"What in the hell for?"

"To line you up. You are one of the nicest men I've ever met. Thank you, and I won't peel potatoes anymore when making hash."

They both laughed.

Packhorse loaded, they started north for her home place. He planned to cut cross country and hit the high road and save the time to go south to Fort McDowell and then come back north on the wagon road. Besides, this was his country, and he knew the land well. He soon saw she was a horse person, and she rode the bay, a natural in the saddle, but he'd bet she'd ridden since she was little.

He took a single packhorse, one of his ranch horses that led easy, and they made good time, forded the Verde River, and headed toward Four Peaks through the bristling cactus and the giant saguaros that studded the rolling hills. He told her to stay out of the cholla—the flying cactus that had a million spines and all barbed. A person could brush close by it, and it would attack them and was nearly impossible to pull off.

Buzzards circled them and then flew on. By afternoon, they were on the Ox Bow Road and headed north. There was little traffic, and they made good time, so they reached Rye that evening.

He asked her where she wanted to camp.

"Away from the curious."

"Let's fill our canteens and my two jugs at the village well. I will buy some grain for the horses in the Rye store. There will not be much graze for them up here. Then we can set up camp and cook something. We have enough daylight left."

"I agree. Jeb, I am sorry I was so hard on you. But I was so upset. Three days of being held prisoner, doped by them, and then breaking loose while I was tied to a saddle horn. I know you had no part in that kidnapping and any abuse I suffered from them, but I am still not certain I can go back home to live my life and not fear someone else will do the same thing all over again."

"Come live with me. They won't find you."

They both laughed. He considered that she hadn't said no outright. He dismounted, went into the store, bought the grain and some hard candy to share with her. The storekeeper thanked him for his business. Outside, he fished out some peppermint. She bent over in the saddle, and he put one in her mouth and one in his.

Her grin and soft thanks were enough to perk him up.

The water containers filled at the well, and the partial sack of grain tied on his saddle horn, they rode off down the broad dry wash and chose a place to camp.

He gathered some dry wood and started a fire. She fixed biscuits to go in the Dutch oven. Beans and coffee water were soon heating. They had some time to sit and wait. No one bothered them or even came by their camp.

The reprieve from the day's push settled him down a lot. He still wondered how old she really was but felt that would be asking a too personal question, and he was a mere guide to take her back home. If she wanted him to know, she'd tell him.

"You ever have a wife?" she asked.

"No. I never really had much to offer one. Plus, there aren't any women—respectable ones, at least—in my neighborhood."

"There are Indians nearby."

"I know a few. I don't speak their language."

"You never met a female one?"

He chuckled. "Not one I wanted up there."

"How many cows do you run?"

"Fifty head now."

"You have about thirty calves to sell a year, then."

"I get a few more than that, and I sell yearlings."

"Can you get forty bucks a head for one?"

"I usually can."

"Then you make a hundred dollars a month."

He nodded. "But I just got up to those numbers. I have done lots of day work at roundup. Hunted down some wolves killing sheep, sold firewood, and guided some hunters. I also have built fence and butchered critters for folks."

"I can't see why some gal hasn't caught you."

"What about you? You aren't married, are you?"

"No." She shook her head. "I am nearly an old maid. I'll be twenty-four in two months.

He shook his head in disbelief. "I'd never guessed it."

Thanks. How old did you think I was?"

"Fourteen, fifteen."

Her shoulders slumped. She asked, "Am I that childish?"

"I have not had much experience being around women in a long time. Why have you not been married?"

"I am real outspoken. I am bossy, and my father says I'm spoiled. Most guys have not wanted me. They wanted my family ranch more than they wanted me. The man I marry may never come along, but he better want me with or without that damn ranch."

"I guess you answered all the questions I had."

"What now?"

"Coffee water's boiling."

She jumped up, brushed off her seat, and went to work. "I can make it. No scorched barley tonight."

He laughed. "I've drunk my share of that."

A coyote yipped off in the brush and another answered. It would be another mild night. After they ate beans and biscuits, they turned in. He gave her a canvas sheet and some blankets. He laid his own roll not far away from her.

He wanted to tell her if she became upset to wake him, but he kept it to himself. She more than likely wasn't interested. At twenty-four, she looked a lot younger. No difference to him. Six years younger than he was—he couldn't believe it.

He woke in the night in a start. His fist clutched his Colt's wooden handle he found under the covers. Something big was shuffling things around. That's what woke him, the rattle of pots and pans. He could make out a good size bear's snuffing at his cooking things—he hoped she had not heard him.

That forty-five Colt might stop him. Might only make it mad too. He needed his rifle in a scabbard across camp. He wasn't a grizzly, but even a black bear could be trouble if wounded.

He recalled an ax he'd laid down. Shoot five shots at him and finish him off with the ax if he was still standing. He eased off the bedroll in a crouch. Six-gun in his fist and the hammer cocked back, he stood up and blasted away.

The bear roared with each bullet striking his body with a smack. Reared up on his hind feet, the bullets did not knock him down or stop his rage. Jeb threw down the pistol, caught the axe handle in his left hand. He swung it with both hands, smashing the axe into the bear's head, and it fell at his feet, growling and whining as it died.

Someone had hold of his arm—squeezing it. "My God, Jeb, you killed him with an ax. I can't believe you're that fierce."

His six-gun holstered, he swung her around and hugged her. "I softened him up with five forty-five bullets."

She squeezed him real tight. "You killed him with an ax. I never saw a man that brave in my life. You did that for me, didn't you?"

"I damn sure didn't want you hurt."

"I can't believe anyone is that tough? You aren't even shaking. I'm shaking more than you are." Her entire body shuddered in his hug.

He exhaled. "You aren't inside me. I can't get my breath. I guess I was too close to death."

He hugged her again, and in a brief flight of his senses, he kissed her forehead. Never knew why. Something that he did on impulse, and next she found his mouth with hers and pulled him down to kiss him harder.

Next, on their knees, they were trying to get enough of each other's mouths and going for it all. Sprawled on top of his bedroll with her under him, he was drowning in kissing, and so was she.

Finally, he braced himself over her, huffing for his breath. "Veronica, I do not want you for your body over me killing a bear, but I sure do want you. I want every part of you, but not because of this bear kill. I want you because you feel free and safe with me in a better world than that stinking bear gave us this morning."

"I am not afraid of you. I am yours, Jeb, if you want me."

"No. Let us make it fun and open. Do it by the rules, and we will have a long happy life. I want you to have a chance to back out if you don't think you could be my wife."

"Let me up."

He frowned at her "You over the notion of us?"

"No silly. I want that stinking bear farther away from us."

He wrestled her down and kissed her some more, but they were both laughing too hard to do anything but at last sit up and get over it.

Afterward, they moved the smelly bear, dragging him across the wash.

When they had him over there, she shook her head "His pelt is no good."

He agreed. "I want his teeth though."

"I won't ever forget him."

"You won't ever forget him?"

Then she hugged him and cried. He didn't know what to do about that but hugged her back.

She took his hand in hers and led him back to their camp as the sun crept over the mountain in the east. "I am a spoiled brat, but, Jeb, I want to share my life with you. I am impressed with you. Not just the bear deal. You are the calmest man I ever met in a crisis and the nicest one too. It won't be easy for you or me, but I want us to be together, and I promise I will do my part."

"That's all a feller could ask of anyone. I don't have the most education, but I don't feel I'm stupid. I like how you figured out my income. You will have to show me that on paper, but I can learn too."

They made oatmeal for breakfast afterward, loaded up, and rode north. He figured they were two days away from where he thought her father's ranch was located.

She asked a lot about his place. Did he have enough water for a household? He assured her that he did. His hand dug well had a good spring source feeding it. He picked it to be his homestead because it had some *tules* growing in some marshes. Cattails were what folks called them. The *tules* were what the natives called them.

"Is there a road into it?"

"Yes, you can get a wagon or buckboard up there."

"I never asked or knew what your brand is?"

He pushed his horse in closer. "The Rafter JS."

"I can remember that easy enough. I was only there a short while, and I was still upset."

"You aren't upset any longer?"

She frowned at him. "No. In fact, hell no. I feel very secure and pleased to be riding with you. I promise you I won't cuss any more, but I never felt more secure in my life. I can even think about tomorrow and the next day. That was something they'd spoiled for me."

"You didn't know them?"

"No. I never saw them before they kidnapped me? I guess they had seen me."

"Hold that for a minute. There are two men up there in the road ahead of us."

"Who are they?"

"I don't know, but be ready for anything. They reined up when they saw us like they knew who we were."

"It may be some of Dad's men looking for us. I mean looking for me."

He took out the field glasses. The pair looked scruffy to him. He handed them to her.

She shook her head and gave them back. "I don't know them."

"It isn't the kidnappers?"

"No."

"I think I can handle them, but be careful."

She squeezed her eyes shut and shook her head. "And I thought all we had to do was ride home."

He pushed his horse ahead and nodded for her to trail him. His six-gun was reloaded, and he considered the Winchester under his right leg. It was too. No reason they'd bother them, but they acted suspicious reining up like they planned to do something when they got to them.

He felt a real tightness in his chest and an urge to get by them as smoothly as possible. But like the bear, he'd take care of them in a similar way if they tried anything.

He reined up fifty feet away from them. "Are you two blocking the road for a reason?"

The one with the white whiskers checked his anxious acting horse. "Free country. You can get by."

"I'd appreciate you moving aside for us to pass." Their tough manner was getting on his nerves.

"That gal with you has a big price on her head. Me and Ernie want half of it."

"You didn't find her." He shook his head, so she didn't speak.

"We have now."

"No. You found a way to get your free ride to hell. Move over or I'm counting both of you as dead."

"Who in the hell are you?"

"Jeb Simms."

"Never heard of you. Huh, Ernie?"

"Naw—" Ernie's jaw dropped at the sight of the cocked gun in Jed's fist pointed at them.

"Stand aside. The reason you have not heard my name is most folks who challenge me have not lived to talk about it. Honey, ride on by them."

She did as he told her.

"Now easy, with two fingers, get those guns out of your holsters and drop them on the road."

They both carefully did as he said. "Don't follow us, or I'll use my rifle on you."

"Mister this ain't going to be our last meeting," white whiskers said.

"What's your name?"

"Cal Rutledge."

"Ernie, what's your last name?"

"Ernie Harris. Why you asking?"

"'Cause we meet again, you'll be dead, and I want your mother to find your grave marker to cry over you."

"You son of—"

He pushed the .45 at Rutledge. "You're asking for it."

The man backed his horse up, shaking his head. He wanted no part of that .45 in Jeb's fist.

By this time, she was well up the road, and he told them he'd see them in hell and rode off to catch her. When he did, they retrieved their pistols and trotted their horses on up the mountain the other way.

She looked back several times. "They aren't coming."

"You know why?' he asked her.

"Why?"

"They don't want to die."

She nodded and smiled. "I'd want no part of you mad either."

"Sidewinders like that don't deserve to walk the earth. Saying they wanted part of the reward business. He was a damn bully and deserved what that bear got last night." He took a deep breath and tried to come off his madness.

"Well, Jeb Simms, I am glad I saw your other side. I won't worry about my safety with you ever again. Now, I will worry bullies like them don't get you."

"Darling, there is always something or some dumb critter like them in this world."

"I like that Texas drawl when you say darling. We are half a day's ride from my father's ranch. With no fears, no things holding me back, tell me our plans."

"I been thinking how I'd hate to marry an old maid and since you will be one in less than two months, you can tell me when we will get married."

"You are supposed to propose."

"I thought I did that last night."

She shook her head.

"Then when we top this mountain, we'll rest the horses, and now you can rehearse telling me your answer."

"No. No. No."

"How many years since you got spanked for being a smart mouth."

"Never."

"First time for everything."

She rode in and slapped his arm. "Hell, yes. You really are fun when you get limbered up. I believe we are going to have a good time at this marriage business."

"A few more characters like those last ones we met, and I won't know what to believe."

They stopped on the mountain pass and dismounted. She came over and hugged him. He stumbled through, "Would you, Veronica Rhodes, marry me?"

"Only—only forever."

Sealed with a kiss, the fresh wind swept them into each other's arms like they'd done that forever. His life was taking on a new road, and he was sure proud. Why he'd never even dreamed to fall into a deal like this—part of the time he wondered if he really was dreaming and these happenings were not reality.

———————

AN ARMED POSSE MET THEM on the road close to the ranch. A big man in charge who must have been their foreman rode in and said, "Thanks we can take her from here."

"Donnie Franks, this man saved my life. His name is Jeb Simms. He is going to be our guest."

"Yes, Miss Rhodes. We're glad you are all right. Where did they take you?"

"Jeb saved me clear down by Fort McDowell."

"How did you get that far?"

"It is too long to tell here. Did you get the pair who kidnapped me?"

"No. They got away. We looked all around here and couldn't find a sign. I think your father thinks they killed you."

Riding along with them, Jeb could tell Donnie Franks didn't put much stock in him. But, hell, he didn't run her life either. He'd see how things went when they reined up at the big sprawling log house.

"Your dad isn't home right now. He will be back later. Simms, you can sleep in the bunkhouse."

"Donnie, this man saved my life. He will be my guest in the main house."

"Whatever you say, but I'm not sure your father will approve."

"He will approve, or I'll know why. Give him your reins. They'll put up the horses," she said in an order like way.

"Nice meeting you, Franks." She put her hand out for Jeb to hold, and they walked that way up to the big house.

"Don't pay him any mind. He thought I'd fall in love with him several years ago. I didn't—he's another of the *I want the ranch* guys."

I watched his actions moving off thinking he might draw and shoot me—or try. "He acted like your father would not approve of me?"

"Hogwash," she said. "See I didn't swear. They can all lump it. Meet Juanita who is the head housekeeper."

A nice-looking Mexican woman in her thirties rushed out on the wide porch to hug her. "Oh, *señorita*, I am so glad you are safe and sound. Who is this *hombre*?"

"The *hombre* saved my life. Jeb Simms. He ranches down by Fort McDowell."

"I am so pleased you saved her life. Welcome to the Rocking R Ranch. Oh, her father will be so proud to have her back in one piece, *señor*. Come, I have food for you two to eat. You must have ridden a long way."

"After food, we both need a bath."

"I can arrange that, *señorita*. I have some clothes that will fit him too."

"Juanita, when father comes, I will tell him. Jeb wants to marry me?"

"Oh, darling, many men have wanted to do that."

"I told him, yes."

"Wonderful. You are a very lucky man, *señor*."

"I thought so too."

"What about your father?" he asked.

"He can like it, or we can go live on your ranch down there."

"I bet he accepts it then."

She made a face and shook her head. "He won't have a choice."

The bath they had for him was hot water and deep. A shaving kit and his clothing to wear were laid out. One of the two maids asked if he needed anything else before they left him. He told her no and thanks. Washed, shaved, and dried he dressed in the fresh clothes. They about fit him, but his suspenders would hold up the pants, so he was fine, and he walked down the hall.

He heard a loud conversation.

"I will pay him a large sum, and he can go back home."

"No, Father, I plan to marry him."

"You need to marry someone of substance. Now Donnie Franks is—"

"I am not marrying your blowhard foreman who only wants me for this ranch. And I will leave here for good if you say one more word about Jeb or against me ever getting married."

I cleared my throat.

"Jeb, I want you to meet my father, Calvin Rhodes." She jumped up and kissed me.

"Nice to meet you, Simms. My daughter here says that you saved her life, and that she wants to marry you."

"Sit back down, sir. I asked her to marry me. I realize you have no idea who I am or how we came to be together."

"I'd hear that story. Have a seat."

He did and to show her commitment to him she sat on his lap. "Well, I was down on the Verde River after taking a bath. She showed up on a reinless horse with her hands tied to the saddle horn and about passed out. I had no idea who she was or what was going on. I made a travois to carry her and took her to my ranch house. She came around from the dope they'd given her, so I fed her, and the next day brought her home.

"My intentions have been honest, and somewhere along the way we kind of took to each other, and I asked her to marry me. She said she would, and I said, fine, I will take you home and ask your father for your hand."

"I don't even know you."

"My pedigree says I'm from a cotton patch Texas family. I took cattle up to Abilene and Wichita, Kansas. Homesteaded a ranch in the McDowell Mountains. I have a herd of cows there now and a registered brand—Rafter JS. That's my story."

"A *wickiup* to live in?"

"No, she's seen it. I have a log house, a cooking range and someday it'll be a real ranch."

She nodded. "I have seen his place, and his hard work shows."

"I think you two should wait six months and see if she really wants to live in your trap."

I put my finger on her protest. "I really think, we can get up and leave, and you can't stop us. Then don't you ever come by to see your grandchildren, because you won't be welcome at our house. One woman left you she said. Another can do the same. I don't think you want that to happen, but I see you either welcome us as man and wife, or we'll saddle up and leave here today."

Rhodes frowned at him. "Veronica, are those your wishes?"

"I said I'd marry him. I intend to keep my word."

There was a long silence. "When?"

"A week?"

"He can go home and come back for it."

"He is not leaving without me, and any JP will marry us along the way."

"Do as you damn well please then."

"Father? He's told you once. We can do this friendly or without."

Rhodes gave a deep sigh of surrender. "We will do it friendly."

"Good." She turned and kissed him. Then they squeezed each other's hands. "Juanita and I will make the plans for our wedding to happen here."

"Yes. I can't say I am glad to meet you, Simms, but welcome to the family." He got up and left us.

"He'll get over it. In the morning, let's saddle some horses and go have a look at the ranch."

"Darling, I'm with you."

Her father's plans were in shambles in Jeb's consideration. What put him on edge was disrupting his plans for his foreman to marry her for the ranch. Her father figured the foremen could run that big ranch when he got older. Jeb was the part that got in their way by picking her a man that didn't suit either of them.

Too damn bad. That even made him want her more. He was not some upstart nobody. By her figures, he made four times a cowboy's pay a month. Probably twice what he paid that stiff shirt foreman of his. Their house would never be as spacious as this big palace, but Rhodes couldn't even keep a wife here. What good did it do him? His wife left anyway.

In the morning, Juanita was in the kitchen making breakfast with another woman and looked shocked to see him up so early.

"Don't worry I just always get up with the chickens."

They laughed. Juanita brought him a steaming cup of coffee and offered him cream and sugar.

"I just drink coffee. Mmm. This is good."

"How did you ever win that girl? I can't believe how much she thinks of you, señor?"

"I was not sure I could turn her head. But we had a bear in our camp coming up here. I shot him, but it didn't kill him, so I had to kill him with an axe."

"You killed a bear with an ax?"

"I ran out of bullets. I had to do something. You do what you have to do when things get that short."

"I am sure impressed."

"Impressed about what?" Rhodes asked, coming into the room.

"*Señor* Simms killed a bear with an axe in their camp."

"Aw—you did what?"

"There was a bear pilfering in our supplies in the night coming up here. There aren't many bears down there in that desert country. I figured he was hungry and dangerous. I put five .45 slugs in him, and he kept coming. All I had left was an axe. I swept it up and split his skull."

"Did you save his hide?"

"He was a mangy stinky old devil. But I knocked out all his teeth to make a necklace."

"You kill many bears with an ax?"

"No, sir, but I had no choice. He had to be stopped."

Rhodes took a seat, and Juanita brought him coffee. "You found her?"

"No, sir. I took a bath in the Verde. Washed my clothes. I got dressed, and here came a horse with a drunk-looking rider. The horse wanted a drink. She wasn't conscious and had her hands tied to the horn. I cut the rope, and the horse went by me to get that drink. I carried her across the river from there. She later told me they doped her. I had no doctor. I made a travois and took her to my place. She ate some oatmeal I fed her, and she went to sleep.

"When she had some strength, we set out to bring her back here."

"You must be one helluva guy. You've damn sure impressed her, obviously."

"Mister Rhodes, I treated her like I would my daughter if I had one."

"I want those SOB's who kidnapped her."

"I never heard of them. I wouldn't know how to look for them."

"I'll find them."

"Oh, I bet you will."

"You're going to make her live over there in some shack."

"That's my place. She won't be shocked. She's seen it."

"I bet you ten bucks that in less than a month she leaves you and comes home where she belongs. She's not some squaw. She's lived her entire life more like a princess. Being a common housewife will soon sour her on being your wife. Mark my words you son of a bitch. She won't stay long with you."

"If this is such a great place to live, why did your wife leave you?"

"Who told you that?"

"Veronica said she left you when she was very young, and no one heard from her again. Why did she leave this palace? Household help? There was a good reason she left here, and it wasn't because she was being treated like a queen. Was it?"

"That is none of your gawdamn business."

"It may become more my business than you think. I don't think you ever tried to find her, did you?"

"That is none of your business."

"I wasn't snooping, but I see you have kept many records of this ranch as you built on it. Show me the folder with the correspondence you kept on that search you never made for her."

"How dare you challenge me?"

"If you did it, fine. I merely want to see the effort you made to find her mother."

"That was twenty years ago. I don't have them."

Jeb shrugged. "She doesn't have to do anything she doesn't want to do with me. I didn't take advantage of her, and I wouldn't. I didn't come here for you to support me, but I still find that story hard to believe. Her mother left a small child of her own in this man's world with no compassion for that child. Did she ever write you?"

"No. She was totally self-centered and wanted no part of anything about this ranch."

"She must have had brothers and sisters. Family back there?"

"Jeb Simms, I don't have to answer one question you ask me. Stay out of my way, or you won't marry her. You will be dead."

Rhodes stalked out of the room. Jeb remained in the living room, and the breeze made the lace curtains sway some. He could see her father down there at the foot of the stairs beating his leg with his large felt hat and shouting at his foreman—no doubt about him. *Too bad.*

In a short while, Rhodes drove a buckboard out the front drive. The dust spiraling away from his wake by the wind.

How could he learn what happened to her mother? That had bugged him since she told him about her disappearance.

"Were you and my father arguing?" she asked swinging on his arm.

"I asked about what he did when your mother left here?"

"I told you—"

"I know. I asked to see that correspondence from when she left and how he tried to find her."

"That bothers you don't it?"

"If you were here and had a little girl. Would you leave her if you planned to leave me?"

"No."

"But you believed what you were told. That she didn't want either of you. You are a part of her, and even you after being raised in an all-male house would not leave a small girl behind."

"I never doubted it."

"Can we find that old file?"

"Maybe."

"If you don't want to know, I will stop."

"No. It may be in the trunk in the attic." She took his hand, and they went upstairs, then up a ladder. He opened a few dormer windows to let some of the heat out.

She opened a steamer trunk and got out a picture in a frame. "This was made the summer before he married her. It was taken in Texas he said."

"You look like her. She was very pretty. They met there?"

"His father had some property in Virginia the U.S. Government wanted, and he traded the U.S. Government for this ranch land. There are sixty sections deeded here."

He whistled. "That is big as some states almost."

"It is a huge ranch. Dad came here after he was discharged from the Army to build it, and I was born here. He sent me east for a while to a school, but I hated it, and when I said I had enough, he let me come home."

They looked through the various folders opening large envelopes. Newspaper stories about her father's service were faded. Obviously, his father was a rich man in New York State, and his son got lots of newspaper attention.

Then he found something. A resealed letter-size envelope among some correspondence. It was stamped from San Antonio, Texas. The date was blurred.

"I am going to open this. All right?"

"Sure."

"It is a letter and an obituary from a newspaper."

He began to read it. "Dear Mister Rhodes. The woman's body we found at the murder scene at one sixty-seven San Rio Street last February was identified as one Margery Rhodes, age twenty-eight. Blue eyes, brown hair. Weight, one hundred fifty pounds. Rhodes was listed as a working prostitute by the San Antonio health department. A sister, Veronica Denton, claimed her property. She said that Margery had no husband or children. That is all I can tell you. The murderer is unknown and may have been one of her clients. I am sorry. I have no more information. If anything turns up, I'll have the officer inform you. And they will respect your privacy. Desk Sergeant John Salazar, Police District Two, San Antonio, Texas."

"So her death was three years after she left the ranch. Were you named for her sister?"

"I must've been. No one told me she had a sister or who her parents were."

"Why didn't they tell you?"

"I guess I never asked. I don't want to, but I may cry, big man." She put her hand on his shoulder, both of them on their knees.

"I didn't want to bring you to tears. The story upset me when I heard it. Maybe I dug too deep."

She clung to him, kissing and weeping. "No, while I have no real answer, it tells me lots."

Jeb heard someone coming up the ladder, coughing and out of breath. It was her red-faced father. "Both of you come downstairs. What did you find?"

"Tell him," she said, sniffing.

"The letter San Antonio police Sergeant Salazar's wrote you."

"The rest is in my office for you two to read. All of it."

Jeb helped her up and hugged her.

Rhodes went down the ladder still coughing.

She put her arms around his neck and kissed him. "You fight bears and things that are wrong the same way. What do you think he has?"

"I hope what I asked for." He went down first to catch her if she missed a rung.

There were letters and papers scattered over the desk. He was seated without a tie or coat by the open window and never spoke a word to them.

They carefully handled the letters reading and handing them back and forth to each other. Then they whispered about the source and information.

...two of the young men in my office talked to her in the barrio about providing her rent in a respectable neighborhood and a monthly stipend if she would divorce you quietly. Her response was too vulgar to include in this letter.

We again contacted her two weeks ago and offered her a lump sum as you directed. She said no.

Unless you have any other plans, my office will suspend contacting her.

Norris Clemens, Senior Partner
Partner in Washington, Legget, and Clemens Law Office

"Let's sit and talk. You two on the couch." He carried the wooden chair over to face them.

"I met your mother in a house of ill repute on a wild spree in Big Springs, Texas. I had just been discharged from the Army and was going west to build this ranch. She impressed me so damn much—I took her to El Paso with me, and we honeymooned in the big hotel for two weeks. Night and day.

"My father sent me a wire to get my butt to Arizona. I think the man we had hired to be my foreman had wired him to ask where I was?"

"That was when that one photograph was taken of her?" she asked him.

"Yes. Wasn't she lovely?"

"You never took another photo?" she asked.

"Some time after she left me, I destroyed all but that one."

"You were mad. I understand."

"Veronica, I was mad. When we were partying and getting drunk in El Paso, she was the perfect companion. But the reality of the ranch life up here made her draw up into a shell. I had no money to run off and raise hell, and there was nothing close. Then we conceived you. That changed her mentally. During the pregnancy I grew to wish we had not done it. I worried she would commit suicide.

"She had some good days after you were born. I about celebrated, but it did not last. She ran away with some guy she talked into it. I think she shared her body with him to get him to take her to Tombstone.

"I went and found her and forced her to come back. Actually, I knew it was over, but my pride—well she simply couldn't leave me was all I could think."

"To get my spite she had sex with some of my cowboys. I gave up and paid her five thousand dollars and told her I would pay for the divorce. There is an agreement on my desk she signed. My father, when he found out about my outlay, he almost took this place away from me over me paying her that much. I was simply too pride filled to tell you this.

"I will swear on a bible I had nothing to do with her demise. You saw the police sergeant's letter. They never found her killer. But she was registered as a whore. Bad judgment, call it pride, I had no choice I thought but to bury it. That was wrong? But you mess up something, and then it piles on you, and it gets worse and worse."

"Did you ever meet her family?"

"Duggan's. No. They lived near Mason, Texas. Her sister Veronica, yes, your namesake. I met her in El Paso a year after she left me. She wanted me to employ her to get Margery to get the divorce and collect the rent and a stipend. I gave her five hundred dollars, but she kept my money and said she couldn't get her to do it."

"Daddy, I am sorry. Jeb did this for me. Not to destroy you or your reputation, but he wanted the truth, and I did too. Now I know, my heart hurts for a man who loved a woman, and she had another life to live."

"This ranch is yours. My father told me he traded for this place so I could build a big ranch when I came home from the war. I built it, but you mean more to me than all the ranches in the U.S. How much do you have at Fort McDowell, Jeb?"

"Fifty cows, six horses, a house with a range and a well."

"Drive the herd up here. Brand their calves for your children with that iron. I will move over."

"You don't have to do that."

"Yes. Juanita has told me this morning she would marry me. We are going to honeymoon in Mexico if we can. They have a revolution going on down there all the time."

"I wondered about you and her for years." She shook her finger at him.

"I thought we were very secret."

Veronica swung her head around like she was dizzy. "No not secret. But I love you both. Will your foreman quit with Jeb in charge?"

"He may. Then Jeb can find him one."

She ran over and hugged Jeb.

"What do you say to him?" Jeb asked her.

"I'd like us to take a honeymoon before anyone knows about this change. And come back and do all those things. Can we do it that way?"

"Certainly." They shook hands with him, then he kissed the fire out of his to be bride.

Her father said, "Are you two satisfied?"

Jeb looked at her with a nod.

She hesitated, then said, "Yes, Father, and I now understand what hell you went through as well."

He began gathering all of it up and putting it in a folder.

"You are going to save it?" Jeb asked him.

"Yes, I will save it. You know you are taking the one thing I hold dear to my heart over this ranch and everything else?"

"Veronica?"

"Yes."

"I'll take care of her."

"We came from different worlds. But obviously you are a determined man and will do things different than I have. No one really knows all the right ways to live.

"When you two get back from your world, we'll talk about my father's large estate he left us and other loose ends that we will have in this world."

"Daddy, we are taking some bedrolls and packhorses to look at the ranch the next few days. My dress will be ready to be fitted on Friday. Juanita says she can handle the party arrangements for our wedding next Saturday. I made her a list of who to invite, you may add anyone to it you want to see here."

"Both of you be careful."

"We will." She stood on her toes and kissed his cheek.

"Don't do anything I would not do."

Jeb heard her quietly add. "With Juanita?"

Then they laughed.

They rode out in the morning. Two fat packhorses loaded down, and they headed north. She wanted him to see many parts of the upper ranch since it stretched into the pines under the Mogollon Rim. The ranch headquarters sat in the elevation. Higher up the Ponderosa Pines grew.

The road split farther north at the place called Junction which had some stores and two saloons. It was where the road split going to Mormon Lake on the west fork of it as well as the railroad town of Flagstaff the real closest town of any size to them. The east fork of that road went to Holbrook and then Gallup, New Mexico. South was Fort McDowell, a Yavapai Indian reservation, then Hayden's Ferry, and beyond that the new capital of the territory, Phoenix.

She drew him a map in the dust that night in camp after supper.

He agreed he could find his way out.

"I know you have been very polite toward me. I will forever owe you for straightening out the past for me. That took as much courage almost as killing the bear, and I am not making little of that. We have no feather bed out here, but in a week, I will be your wife—so what could it matter?"

"I accept those terms. I have never done it before, so I don't know what to expect. Is that honest enough for you?"

"Me neither, but I want to do it with you. I bet we can figure it out tonight."

And they did.

Somehow afterward it changed everything. Next morning, she sang songs he knew while cooking breakfast. Suddenly it was not her and him. They were one.

Sitting cross-legged on the ground eating her oatmeal and sipping good coffee he kept smiling at her. Damn what a discovery. All this time he'd been alone building a ranch. That all changed with her becoming his wife. She brought an empire for him to look after.

"You pleased or displeased with me?"

He frowned at her. "Hell's bells. I am happier than a pig in the sunshine. We may not get much looking done, but I think our union was glorious."

She bobbed her head, embarrassed. "That was the best part of all this. Just a few days ago I was doped up and feared being raped any minute by those two grimy outlaws. But while they talked big about doing that to me, they never tried. They were so afraid and on the move all the time.

"When their ransom meeting failed because our foreman had set it up to shoot them down with telescoped rifles. They discovered it and fled. If he'd simply given them the money and got me free, they could have run them down. I was so mad that day and finally managed to escape them myself."

He hugged her shoulder. "But then I'd have never found you."

"You are right, and if you hadn't, I'd have been a sassy old maid for sure the rest of my life."

"I figure your foreman will leave when we get married."

She nodded she'd heard him. "No doubt he thought I'd eventually marry him."

"He must be good at his job?"

"Some ways, yes, some ways, no. I think he operates by fear. I mean the ranch hands don't do things because it is best for the ranch. They do it to save being balled out by him."

"I won't say anything about it, but if you are right, and I imagine you are, I will change that. That place needs to be their place. A cowboy finds a cow having trouble he should stop and help her all he can or get help, not ride by fearing he won't get a task done that is what he was sent for."

She was in his face. "I like how you think, big man." She kissed him. "There are still things I have not had enough of that involve you."

———————

TWO DAYS LATER THEY RODE into Junction. He went into the store and bought two cans of peaches. Sitting on the stoop of the covered porch they each ate their can of peaches and said howdy to the customers going by."

One lady asked, "Aren't you Veronica Rhodes?"

"For a short while," she said with a smile. "Saturday, I will be Veronica Simms. This is my husband to be, Jeb Simms."

She waved him from getting up. "No need for you to get up. I have to go home. My Jersey heifer is fixing to calf, and my husband is gone working for a neighbor. My name is Mira Haycox. So nice to meet both of you."

"You have any trouble, we aim to camp down on that marsh this afternoon. Come get me. I can help you."

"Why thanks, Mister Simms. That is a mighty fine offer, and both of you have a grand marriage."

Jeb thought no more of it until midafternoon. A barefoot boy of twelve or so came to their camp and asked if he was Mr. Simms.

He told him he was.

"Well, Missus Haycox can't get that bugger out of her heifer and said you might help her."

"Let me saddle my horse."

The boy shook his head. "Naw it is just over the hill. I'll run tell her you're coming."

He smiled at his wife to be. "Come on it's just over the hill. That way."

She pulled on her boots, and they followed the youth's path over the hill.

He could hear the heifer bawling in pain and could see the tops of the lady's farmstead. The way downhill was steeper through the tall pines than going up. She slid on her butt and laughed when he caught her.

"Why darling it is just over this mountain."

"Next time we'll saddle the horses."

He agreed.

Out of breath, they arrived, and he took over the chore of pulling the calf. She had the small rope tied above his two hooves showing. The poor Mrs. Mira Haycox looked soaked with sweat through and through plus covered in straw from wrestling with the job.

He sat on his butt, boots planted on the heifer's butt and strained.

"He's coming, Mira."

"Good. I guess me and the boy together didn't have enough pulling power."

The slick calf slid out and bawled. He struggled around and Jeb took the ropes off his legs. "Little man, you and Momma will make it now."

He tailed the heifer up, and she went to licking her calf.

"What do I owe you?"

Veronica interceded, "He won't charge you a thing. Will your husband be home Saturday?"

"No, he will be home tonight. But I can pay you two."

"What is his name?"

"George Haycox. Why?"

"Get this boy to watch your stock, have George load up some things in a wagon on Friday, drive down to our ranch, and stay in my house. Saturday you will be at my wedding as my special two guests."

"Oh, we couldn't do that."

"I am only getting married once in my life. I want you there."

"He hasn't a suit to wear."

"Our cowboys will be there. They don't have suits. You come."

"I will try, Veronica."

"Good. See you Friday at the ranch."

———————————

JEB SIMMS WORKED HARD ALL his life improving the large ranch with his wife, Veronica. Beside three lovely children they expanded the operation and size of the Rhodes Ranch to quadruple the size, so when their sons, Rod and Bert, began operating it, theirs was one of the top ten cattle ranches in the state of Arizona, and they were recognized nationally as conservationists.

Jeb told a reporter who interviewed him on his eightieth birthday and asked him how did he ever get to be such a big rancher.

"Son, I guess by just minding my own business."

———————————

JEB AND MIRA LEARNED A few years after the incident happened, how Apache had killed the two men who had kidnapped his wife while they were making their escape from her father's men. That knowledge made him wonder how his life might have turned out had they not pulled that stunt. His wife casually said, "You'd have died an old bachelor on that hillside ranch. Now, wouldn't that have been a big loss for me?"

They both laughed.

FINDING
WHITE ELK

HE SLIPPED OUT OF THE saddle, the Spencer Repeating Rifle an extension of his right hand. His moccasin soles found solid dirt. A quick check told him nothing looked out of place. Only the laughter coming from under the bank and the sound of the river rushing over rocks broke the silence. He left the crop-eared buffalo pony ground tied and slipped silently to the cutbank's edge. Using some box elders for cover, he dropped on his haunches and pushed his weather beaten wide brimmed hat back on his shoulders—caught at the throat by a rawhide cord.

The sight of the sleek-brown, lithe bodies splashing knee-deep in the stream brought a smile that creased his sun scarred white lips. By damn, he'd sure enough found him a fine-looking mess of red hussies, naked as Eve. He drew in a deep breath at the sight of them. Nothing finer than prime Indian women and there were five of them for him to savor and all of them sure enough fancy maidens. Course he couldn't use more than one—two wives always fought. He'd found that out from the past. One was hard enough to please half the time. The only thing now was how he'd cut out the one he wanted from that herd and carry her off.

Oh, the gal he finally picked out would have a fit like a wild horse when he first snatched her up. Couple days they'd tame down like a mustang did and accept their fate—from there on she'd be his woman. It was the Indian way to take a wife. Then they'd set in like a white woman wanting things and complaining the wood wouldn't burn or the campsite was in a poor place. He even missed that ranting since he'd buried One Braid. His red mule had kicked her in the head over a month earlier—poor girl, but she never opened her eyes after the mule planted a swift hoof to her skull. Breathed for about a half day and moaned in a coma in his arms most of that time. Nothing he could do for her but rock her in his lap and talk nice to her till she died. He swallowed a knot in his throat. One of these Ree women would do fine.

The one that looked kind of dignified. Held her head up when some of the others tried to dunk her, and she out maneuvered them. Two of them short ones, they'd be too fat for his liking in no time on his rations. The other two were too thin to be appealing. Besides she was the proudest looking one of them all—that would be his first choice.

He started back for the dun-colored horse he called Feathers. Their camp was a good distance. By his plan, he ought to be able to sweep his pick of the lot up, put her belly down over his lap, and make a clean get away. Course some buck who might have had his eye on her could try to track them down. There always was an easy chance of dying in this country. Hell, he'd lived with that for two decades.

At fifteen, he left his family's farm in Illinois to set out to trap and see the entire frontier. No one back there would ever recognize him from the scrawny kid who left home with a poke on a stick over his shoulder when he lit out for the west. Born Elroy Farrel Dirkson. Not long after he left them, he shortened it to Roy Dirk.

He gathered Feathers's jaw bridle rein. In the saddle, he turned him around and set out to where he could enter the river and charge at them. A wave of anticipation went through his shoulders, and he felt excitement grip his innards. The rifle in the scabbard, the sleeves of his buckskin fringed shirt pushed up for action, he set the bay off the bank.

When he hit the shallows, he turned him to the left and set his heels to his ribs. The screams of the panicked females filled the air. The buffalo pony must have known his purpose. He doubled his speed and swept him up to the flushed women. Using his knees to guide the horse, he bent over and caught the one he wanted under the arms and jerked her up over his legs. Water flew in his face, but he tucked her struggling naked wet form across his lap. With her pinned down, he turned Feathers toward the far bank. She kicked and screamed, but there wasn't much else she could do because he held her in place with his left arm.

At last, his pony's hooves struck the gravelly shore. He turned his pony east and set out over the bottoms. He glanced down to admire his thrashing brown prize. With only a moment to satisfy his pride, he drove his heels in Feathers's sides. No place there to let up—time to get the hell out of the Ree's country.

A few hours later, he hauled the lathered, hard breathing horse into a grove of bull pines off the edge of the rolling plains to let him catch his breath. He set the sulking squaw on her feet and stepped down right behind her.

Five feet tall with the nostrils of her narrow nose flared to take in more air. Her eyes shone dark as coal to stare at him with defiance. Arms folded over pear shaped breasts, bare feet set apart, her killer looks at him would have wilted weaker men, he decided. From his saddlebags, he produced a store-bought, blue-checkered dress and tossed it at her. "There, put it on."

She caught it, and not taking her gaze from him, quickly slipped into it. In her haste, she buttoned up the front all-wrong.

"Gods, woman—" he said and caught her by the arm. Then holding her tight so she couldn't escape, he undid the buttons one handed. With her standing tall, he let go and redid them right. The dress was a little big fit, but at least she had clothes on her.

She blinked at him in disbelief. He turned away, fetched a brass telescope out of his saddlebags and using the seat of his saddle for a brace, scoped the plains they'd crossed.

"What's your name?"

No reply.

He turned and looked mildly at her. "What's your name?"

"My—name—Blue Water."

"You a Ree?"

She shook her head.

"You a captive?" He glanced back again.

She nodded.

"Who are your people?"

"Pawnee."

"How in the hell did you ever get up here in Montana?" He re-scoped the plains for any sign. Nothing but some antelope.

"Cheyenne take me as little girl. Army take me away from them. I go to Indian school. Then one day, three Ree girls say they are leaving that place. We steal horses and go away to find their people."

"Do you have a man?"

She shook her head and wrinkled her nose. "No one wants Pawnee woman, but old men."

"My name is Roy." Maybe she meant him—Lordy, he wasn't that old.

"Roy."

"Roy." Nothing out there he could see. He nodded and collapsed the scope.

Her shoulders thrown back, she straightened. "What you want Pawnee woman for?"

He pointed at her. "You're my woman."

"I rather be Ree captive."

"You ain't got lots of choices. Being a Pawnee and a slave, they might not even send anyone after you."

"When they come back from big hunt—"

He nodded. Good news—the men were gone hunting. That might mean they would be days picking up his tracks if they even bothered.

"You can ride behind me or over my lap."

She nodded her head slow like. "Ride behind."

Glad they had that settled, he'd hauled that hellion One Braid three days over his lap after he caught her and busted her back side a dozen times for acting up like he would have a spoiled kid. This one even spoke English. One Braid always addressed him in Sioux and chewed on him like some sergeant in the Army. She'd rant till he finally laughed at her, then she'd grab something at hand and attack him. Damn he'd miss her—maybe this Pawnee would fill in the cracks.

They rode Feathers hard southward and crossed the Musselshell by sundown. They wound up at his cabin long after the moon rose. The paint mare nickered to him when they rode up, and his dogs circled wide of them in the starlight.

"We're home," he said and reached back to set her down.

"No!" She slapped his arm. "I don't want to be bit."

He looked around and laughed. "They won't bite you less I say so."

"You sure?"

"Sure as I am about you."

"What is that?"

"You're going to make me a real woman."

"What if I kill you when you sleep?"

"Why? I give you a new dress. I don't beat you?" He reached back and swung her down.

When the dogs came close to sniff this strange female, she screamed and bumped into his back trying to get away from them. He looked around from undoing the sweaty girths and saw the dogs falling over each other after being spook by her scream.

"Take off his bridle." He gave a head toss for her to do that with his hands full of saddle and pads. "Them damn dogs ain't no threat to you."

Indian dogs were more like wolves than any dogs he knew from his youth. Half wild, they caught their own food or starved. They clung to humans like they'd been cut out from the wolves—but still never acted like real dogs. They'd slink around and cower when caught as if they feared a beating. Tough lot, but they'd bite anyone who sneaked up on his place or if he sicced 'em on them. One Braid butchered most of the puppies when they were milk fat—she ate them by herself, and he didn't reckon Blue, being a Pawnee, would eat them either. He never had no desire for *ala* puppy stew and made it plain right off to One Braid—he'd have none of it.

Besides trading with the various tribes that came down on the Musselshell to hunt buffalo, he still trapped. But anymore, he could buy furs cheaper than he could catch them. A few gee-gaws would fetch a good ermine or mink hide that would have cost him days of zero cold working a trap line. But he was fair with them. That's why so many came by his place to trade. He never cheated a customer.

He put some sugar in the corn bread mix he fixed in a skillet and set it in the fireplace to bake. Sweetness spooned in an Indian woman came out in good measure toward the giver. He had some deer loin cooking over the fire and some dried apples for dessert. Most women like her didn't know what loin even tasted like—the Indian men ate it. Females got rump roast or the ribs.

He'd made her sit on the grizzly skin and face the fire. He wanted to talk to her while he cooked—measure what he must do to make her his woman.

"You ever want to go back and see your people? The Pawnee?" he asked on his knees at the fireplace tending things.

"Some day when I can go in an elk skin dress with many elk teeth,"

"Go over there and look in that trunk." He'd show her the material for one. She frowned.

"Ain't no trap. Go look in that trunk."

"What is there?"

He drew in his breath, cut her a mean impatient look, and she moved quickly to obey. Her first wide-eyed reaction to the contents drew a smile to his lips—she wasn't near as ornery as One Braid was at the start.

"Oh!" she cried out and raised the snowy tanned elk skin out of the trunk. She pressed it to her cheek and smiled like one did holding a pet.

"Could you go back to your people wearing that?"

She blinked her eyes and let it slip from her hands. "You are bribing me. What for?"

With her shoulders back, chin stuck out, she looked ready to be shot—dared him to do it.

He dropped his gaze to the meat cooking over the red-hot coals that spit the drops of grease falling on them. The room, stacked half full of barrels, crates, and hide piles, soon filled with the rich aroma of browning venison. "My woman can wear that as her dress."

She sat down again cross-legged on the bear. "What if I say no?"

"You know there's a big difference between a wife and a slave?"

A slow nod as she bent forward and ran her fingers through the long silky fur of the prime grizzly. She acted as if in deep thought. "You kill this bear?"

"Yes, why?"

"Not many men live to kill such a big animal. They usually kill the man."

"I've killed six grizzlies."

She nodded and still testing the fur under her palm as she swept it back and forth, she looked up at him. "They should call you Many Bears, not Roy."

"I would let my wife call me that."

Again, her head bobbed—not for yes, but more like she had heard his words and took them under advisement. He turned back, and with a leather glove for a potholder, fetched the pan of corn bread out on a bark tray. Using his great knife, he cut it into pie shaped pieces. Then rising to his right knee, he brought out the strips of tenderloin from the grill bars over the fire.

Next, he rose with some effort and took the coffee pot off the iron hook in the fireplace. On his feet, he poured it into two cups and indicated one was for her. She crawled over and recovered it with both small hands holding the tin cup and sat back on her feet. With care she first blew, then sipped some.

"I have drunk coffee before."

"Good, you like it?" He sat down again.

"Maybe when I drink it all I can say."

"Too damn hot right now for anything. This is your food," he said and scooped out a few chunks of the yellow corn bread on the tray with a large portion of meat. Then he handed it to her.

She nodded and moved back from the fire. Holding the platter, she looked at it and then at him for what he would say next.

He took the cue. "Wives eat with their white man husbands. Slaves eat outside later."

"What do you wish me to do?"

"Eat like you're a wife and see how that is."

His words suited her, and she scrambled back to cross-legged. Something in her movements under the dress told him she was an athlete. Some Indian women were very clumsy. Even sober they stumbled all the time. One Braid had not been clumsy, but this Pawnee reminded him of a mountain lion with her lithe movements.

They ate until most of the food was gone, sharing nods of approval, licking their greasy lips, and few words were said. At last finished, he threw his hands back and leaned on them. She scooped up his platter and hers and carried them to the dry sink.

He removed an old briar pipe from his possibles bag and tamped in tobacco. Then on his knees to get close enough, he lit a splinter in the fire and puffing hard soon began to make smoke. Back again on his butt with his knees askew and using them to brace up his fringed arms, he inhaled, then blew the smoke out of his mouth. The nicotine relaxed him and made him feel more comfortable. Been a long three days—to locate her—but even at that, he'd been lucky to find her so quickly.

She rose, facing the flames and the orange firelight danced on the blue-checkered dress. She raised her chin, and the highlights of red shone on her smooth face. With shaking fingers, she undid the first button and paused as if uncertain, then undid two more. The light reflected off her partially revealed breasts as she continued until the garment was open down the front and exposed her flat stomach and the indentation of her navel.

Slowly she began to shrug off the cotton dress. First her smooth brown shoulders shown in the fireplace's glow, then her upper arms, and she turned slightly toward him.

"In your lodge I will be White Elk." She again raised her chin and swallowed hard with her arms pressed against her sides. She held the dress up to cover her nipples from view. "Where does the wife of Many Bears sleep?"

WEST OF THE BORDER

December 12, 1848

THE BIG MAN STOOD IN his stirrups. His hand shielding the glare, he appraised the vast sea of brown bluestem prairie. Below him, the wide Grand River shone in the weak winter sun. Along the water course in the leaf bare trees sat a rectangle of cabins forming a military outpost, Fort Gibson, Indian Territory. Prie Moore rubbed the back of his neck, hunched his tired shoulders, then he checked the restless red mule under him by jerking on the bit.

"Easy, Joshua, we've done made near the last mile to here. That's the place down there you and I've been looking for nigh on to six weeks. Let's go see what Colonel Randolph Hemming knows that we don't." He booted the mule off the hill in a long jog trot.

He was dressed in a black wool suit coat and matching pants, knee high moccasins of deer skin, a red sash around his waist, a once white shirt, a gray silk bandanna around his neck, and a floppy, brimmed felt hat. The man behind those whiskers and collar-length brown hair could have been anywhere between thirty and forty years old. Two single shot cap and ball revolvers rode in his waist band, and a huge Bowie knife was holstered on his right side. In his saddle boot, he carried a double barrel twelve-gauge scattergun.

Through the fort's open gate and across the parade grounds to the commander's office, he came on a short lope. There he reined up, dismounted, hitched the hard-breathing mule at the rack, and tipped his hat to the two bored-looking guards with their muskets and bayonets at ready arms.

"Colonel in?" he asked softly, and the sentry on the right, a freckle faced Irish kid, nodded to him.

"Appreciate it." He went across the flagstone porch, opened the door, and stepped inside the heated office. Standing before the young lieutenant, busy writing in the daily log with a feathered pen, Prie cleared his throat.

No response.

Prie's right hand swept up the great knife. In an instant, the recent graduate of West Point found the sharp tip under his chin, forcing his face up to meet Prie's gaze.

"I'm here to see the colonel."

"He—he—"

"He'll see me. The president of these United States sent me to see him." The lieutenant made a small series of nods that he understood, careful the knife's point didn't gouge the soft skin under his chin. His pen set aside, in a sign of surrender his hands were open and held above the desktop. His hazel eyes continued to widen, and the color drained from under his whiskerless face.

"What's going on out here?" A gray-haired man with deep blue eyes demanded from the office doorway. His uniform coat was unbuttoned, and he wore a usual shabby look about him.

"Me and this West Pointer here had us a small disagreement, Colonel." Prie withdrew his knife and swiftly holstered it. "But it's over now. President James Polk sent me to see you, Colonel Hemming."

"Who?" Hemming batted his eyes in disbelief looking him over.

"President James Polk. May we go into your office and talk privately?"

"You all right, Olsen?" Hemming asked his junior officer.

"Fine, sir."

With a hard look written on his ashen face, the colonel turned back to Prie.

"Come into my office, but I'll warn you now. If this is a hoax, there'll be hell to pay."

From the inside pocket of his coat, Prie removed the letter wrapped in oilskin.

He waited for the man to assign him to a chair before the polished desk. No doubt this expensive fixture had been shipped to the frontier at some great expense to the Army.

"Be seated. Lieutenant Olsen, come in here and take notes of this meeting."

"Yes, sir."

Prie held out the letter toward the colonel.

"You know what we do with impostors out here?" Hemming asked, glaring across at him before taking the folded parchment.

"I am certain it's dreadful. My business here is explained in that letter." Prie nodded toward it.

Hemming glanced at the paper, scowled, and then handed it to his man, holding his iron gaze on Prie. "Here, Olsen, you read it—aloud."

"Yes, sir," Olsen began. "It says Colonel Randolph Hemming, Commander, Fort Gibson, Indian Territory.

"This letter is to introduce my special agent, Priely Moore. You are to assist him in all ways necessary for him to complete his assignment. His job as a special presidential agent is to bring to the bar of justice two of the worst scoundrels and murdering felons on the face of the earth, Hargo Donaghue and Lance Gunther. Should Moore need any monies, supplies, animals, armament, or even companies of men, you are to supply them. His signature for those needs is sufficient for your quartermaster's report. Moore is a resourceful individual, but should he need your help, you are to provide all of his needs. My regards to you and all the fine young men serving out there on our western frontier.

"Sincerely Yours, James Polk, Commander-in-Chief, President of the United States of America."

"My, my, you must be some important man." Hemming frowned as if taken aback, and when his man handed it back to him, he reread the letter to himself.

Prie ignored the man's comments. "You know these two men I'm after?"

"No. But I suspect someone around the fort does if they're in the country. How did you get here, anyway? By river?"

"No, I rode a mule. I left St. Louis six weeks ago."

"You must have a helluva fast mule." Hemming gave him a questioning gaze, ready to pour some whiskey in two glasses taken from his desk drawer.

Prie moved forward in his chair and glared at the man. "I do, and that means, if you don't get to doing something quick about getting me some answers, I'll ride that mule back up there and have the orders cut to assign you to the Mexican border. You can command some isolated post down there."

"You think that would be worse than this hell hole?" Hemming laughed aloud at his threat.

"Lots worse. Now, send for someone who knows where they are or where I can find them."

"Olsen, send four men out and bring in Nate Tenhorse. Make it five men."

"Yes, sir."

"Wait," the colonel said. "He's not in the brig, is he?"

"No, sir."

"Who's this Nate, anyway?" Prie asked.

"Nate Tenhorse. He's a Cherokee scout. Have some whiskey. It'll calm you down some."

"Isn't he—this scout attached to the fort?"

"The damned Army won't give me enough funds for that. I can only hire them by the day when I'm chasing hostiles."

Prie shook his head in disgust, then downed some of the whiskey. He held up the glass to the light and examined it. "Not half bad for this far from civilization."

Hemming relaxed at last, slouched in his wheel-back chair that creaked in protest. "My private stock. How did you ever get to be a presidential agent?"

"I was a federal revenue agent in Tennessee, and one day, I got called to Washington D.C., and next thing I knew, I was talking to the president."

"You must have been a heckuva agent."

"I got the job done. Tell me something. You're sending five enlisted men to find this Tenhorse guy?"

Hemming nodded.

"Why so damn many?"

"At times he's hard to persuade."

"What is he?"

"Half wild cat and the other half's stubborn as a mule."

"Why put him off on me?"

"'Cause if anyone can find Donaghue and Gunther in this region, Tenhorse can find them."

"Sounds all right then. In the meanwhile, where can I get a bath, shave, haircut, and my clothes cleaned?"

"One of the washer women on the row. What else?"

"Get my mule re-shod?"

"Sergeant Grady at the stables. More whiskey?" Hemming held the bottle toward him ready to pour.

He dismissed it with a headshake. "No thanks, but I reckon that you're thinking this Tenhorse is drunk, right?"

"Yes."

"I thought whiskey was illegal in this territory."

"You want to tax it?"

"That ain't my job anymore."

"It's illegal all right, but it gets in here, and no way I can stop all of it."

Prie said, "I will get a bath and the rest, and I expect that scout to be here by then."

"You are a very impatient man. He will be here by then."

Prie stopped at the doorway and glared back at the man. "That's what I expect."

A soldier directed him to Helga, a thick waisted German woman, who provided him with a wooden tub and a hot bath inside her small cabin. Afterward, she seated him on a stool. Wrapped in a feed sack towel around his waist while his clothes dried, she gave him a haircut and peeled six weeks of whiskers off his face, a skill she no doubt learned scraping butcher hogs at killing time.

Dressed at last, he paid her four bits and left her biting down hard on the coins with her eyetooth to ensure they were real. He crossed the parade yard leading Joshua to the post's blacksmith. Despite the cool temperature, the man with his massive, muscled arms wore a sleeveless shirt as he beat with vengeance upon a cherry-red rod atop his anvil. Some sweaty faced private worked the bellows keeping his forge coals glowing. The big man looked up at Prie's approach.

"You Grady?"

"Ya, why?"

"The colonel said for you to re-shoe my mule."

The farrier closed one blue eye and glared hard at him. "Where's he at?"

"Josh is right here."

"I don't mean the mule. I mean the colonel."

"In his office I guess. Why?"

"Cause I'm going to shove this poker up his—"

"Listen soldier, you got a beef with him, it ain't with me. Shoe my mule."

Grady dropped the hot iron in a sizzling bucket of water. "And if I don't—"

Color drained from the man's face. The sharp tip of Prie's knife was under his chin as he straightened with guarded movements. "Yes, sir, he'll be ready in two hours."

"One hour and do it right the first time."

"One—" The blacksmith swallowed hard.

"I'll be back for him then." Prie put away the Bowie.

Some sort of tussle was going on down by the main gate. Several soldiers were piling in on somebody. The one in the center was sending them out as fast as they came back in. Fists and boots flew with enough cursing to turn the air blue.

"What's going on over there?" Prie asked.

"They've got old Tenhorse, or he's got them." Grady laughed aloud and nodded to his helper. "Having a helluva good one this time."

"That's Nate Tenhorse?"

"Himself."

"Good." Prie set out for the free-for-all.

"Have him ready in an hour," he said over his shoulder. Then he began pushing soldiers aside. "Hold it right there!"

His voice of authority stopped the others who had formed a circle around the one sitting on his butt. Prie saw a small man with a rat like mustache and two brown eyes that could burn holes in armor steel. His greasy black hair hung in his face, and his chiseled, high cheekbones made him look tough. Dressed in rags, his bare brown feet were mud coated.

"You Tenhorse?"

With a toss of his head to clear back some of the hair, he inspected Prie from head to toe.

"Who in the hell are you?"

"You're new boss."

"Like hell you are." In a fit to get up, two soldiers roughly shoved him back down.

"You have two choices, work for me and get paid, or sit in the stockade until I get back."

Tenhorse turned his head to the side and looked hard at him. "When're you getting back?"

"I have no plans to return here."

"Who in the hell are you anyway? You ain't no blue boy."

"Your new boss, Prie Moore. Now, tell me where I can find Donaghue and Gunther."

Tenhorse closed his eyes, dropped back on his hands planted behind his back, and shook his head. "Probably over around Fort Smith last I heard of 'em."

"Good, we'll go there. Get the quartermaster to issue you a saddle horse, two pack animals, a bedroll, food for three weeks in the field, a rifle, some ammo, and a tent." Prie glanced down and scowled at other man's bare feet. "Where are your shoes?"

Tenhorse looked as if he'd struck a chord of his dignity. "I've got some."

"Good. What do they call you?"

The guttural words for his name in Cherokee spilled out of the man's freshly split lip.

"Nate will do, mine's Prie."

"Hey, where will you be—when I get all this crap."

"At the blacksmith's." Prie pointed Grady out to him. "In one hour."

"Army ain't that damn fast," Nate said, his voice ringing after him. The soldiers in ear shot horse laughed at his words.

"Mention my name, they will be." He never broke his stride headed for the sutler's cabin

"All right, Prie Moore!" the scout shouted after him, then let out a blistering set of cuss words at the soldiers that had brought him in.

Amused at his outrage, Prie stepped inside the trader's cabin. A small bell signaled his entrance, and a willowy woman in calico came from the rear to wait on him. She made a small curtsy. "And what do you need, sir?"

Not pretty. Not whorish. Not genteel. Her pale complexion was floured with rice powder—wide blue eyes and her red mouth made a natural *O*. She wore her brown hair pinned up in a bun behind her head.

"I want a dozen good cigars and a couple boxes of torpedo head matches for a start."

"My, my," she drawled. "You—are a new one here."

"Yes, ma'am." He tried on a stiff brimmed hat off the shelf.

"Looks mighty good on you." She smiled and, as if shy, looked away in an alluring fashion.

"Won't be that stiff after a good rain on it." He gazed at himself in the small mirror she handed him.

"Oh, it's a good one."

"How much?" He balancing the hat up and down, testing the brim.

"Five dollars."

"Whew."

"This is Fort Gibson, Indian Territory."

"Who's got five dollars in this place?"

"You do." With that, she sashayed off after his other things, making sure he watched her retreat.

"So you're the Missus?" he asked, sniffing the rich aroma of a cigar before she wrapped them in oilcloth.

"Aye. I am."

"Shame."

"Why?" With a look of anticipation, she waited for his reply.

He laughed aloud. "Oh, if I had time today—" Then he shook his head as if disappointed by the constraints of his plans.

"And?"

"How much is my bill? I've got lots of things waiting on me."

"Maybe they ain't so important as... *other* things. Seven dollars if'n you need the hat?"

In a flash, he bent over and kissed her on the mouth. "Cheap enough." Then he put the money on the counter.

Her eyes popped open. The back of her hand flew to her lips like they were burned. Slow like, she shook her head at him as one did at a naughty boy. "Who are you, anyway?"

"Prie Moore, and I'll be going now." He put on the new hat and picked up the old one in his hand to take with him. "What's your name?"

"Julie Judson." And not taking her gaze off of him, she whisked by and opened the door with a bow. Her cheek pressed to the edge of the board door, she looked up longingly at him as if to say, *oh, please sweep me along with you.*

"You're a on beautiful prairie rose in this hellhole, Julie Judson. God take care of you. girl."

"Come back again, Prie Moore," she called after him. Then she dropped her voice almost to a whisper. "Any time. Night or day."

His second meeting with the commander proved less adversarial than the first one. With a broad scrawl, he signed six blank receipts to cover whatever Tenhorse had secured.

"Headed for Fort Smith, huh?" Hemming asked.

"Tenhorse says so."

"Good luck. You know you could have stopped there first. Take my word, it and Van Buren are two more stinking rat holes in this God forsaken wilderness."

"They sound interesting." Prie shook the man's hand.

"You know you'll need lots of luck to ever capture that pair."

"I don't need luck. I just need to get on their trail." He prepared to leave.

Hemming chuckled. "If I were them two and knew you were after me, I'd be shivering in my boots right now."

"If they do that, it's sure fine with me."

"Who's that hat for?" The colonel motioned to the old one in his hand.

"For my scout. It may rain."

"Or snow."

Prie agreed with a curt nod and left headquarters. From the front porch he could see Joshua shining like polished red oak wood in the sun, hitched at the rack out front of the shop. He walked around him making sure the freshly shod mule stood flat on all four hooves.

"Suit, yuh?" Sergeant Grady asked, standing in the open doorway, folding his massive arms over his chest.

"Suits me." They exchanged nods and the man went back inside.

Prie undid the reins, led Joshua, and went to find his scout and outfit. By the warehouse, the Cherokee squatted in the sun with a saddle horse and two more under packs nearby.

Prie tossed him the hat. "Here's your Christmas present."

Tenhorse caught it and inspected his gift. Then he swept his hair back and stuck it on. "I was wondering what you'd get me."

"Too big?" Ready to get in the saddle, Prie checked the girth.

"Just right," Tenhorse said, poking a hole in the hat with his knife.

With a frown, Prie looked over the saddle at him. "What're you doing?"

"Fixing it for a tie down. You don't want me to lose my present the first day?"

"No. Let's ride."

"I'll catch up. Got to fix this hat first."

Prie's eyes closed, he shook his head in disapproval, but he waited.

———————

TWO DAYS LATER THEY RODE through Shack Town across the roiling Arkansas from Fort Smith. On the high sandy bank amongst the bare sycamore and walnut trees, a settlement of breeds, castoffs, and riff raff lived inside the Indian Territory beyond the state's arm of the law. They squatted in old tents, hide covered huts, shacks, and log fronted dug outs. Cooking fire smoke slithered around the ground like a lizard. The rag-clothed women wrapped in tattered blankets stirring their iron pots, looked up with hard-eyed, suspicious stares to study the two men when they rode by them.

"Mary Yellowtail may know something about those two. I'll only be a minute," Nate promised and dismounted. He rapped on the log dugout's rough-sawn board door.

A small boy of five opened it and smiled big. "You Father Christmas?' he shouted at the scout.

"Hell, no! Where's your mother?"

The boy, bare footed and his pants too short for wintertime, circled the Cherokee, scowling indignantly at him. Then his eyes bugged out at the sight of Prie on the mule.

"You Father Christmas?"

Prie could see Nate was talking to an Indian woman in the doorway. He dismounted and dropped to his haunches. "No, but I know him. You looking for him?"

The boy kept searching around and finally looked back at Prie. "Do you really know him?"

"Father Christmas? Sort of."

"Good. Will you tell him Johnny Yellowtail wants to see him?"

"Get back here, Johnny," his mother said and slapped her leg for him to obey.

Prie raised his hand to reassure her. "We're just talking. He's fine."

"Oh," she said warily and shook her head. "He's gone crazy about that Father Christmas business."

When Nate finished talking to her, he came over. "She thinks Donaghue may be in Fort Smith. As for Gunther, he's across the river in Van Buren, last she heard."

"Sounds good enough." Prie turned back to Johnny. "When I see Father Christmas, I'll tell him what all you want."

As if satisfied, the boy nodded and thanked him. His mother shook her head as if he was impossible and herded him back inside the dugout.

"We going after them two now?" Nate asked.

Prie looked at the crude house and used his tongue to search his teeth. "Naw, they won't go anywhere. We're going to Fort Smith to find a rocking horse, some dried apples, and a sack of hard candy."

"But you were the one in such an all-fired big hurry—" The scout blinked his dark eyes in disbelief at Prie.

"When you were small, did you ever wish Father Christmas would come to your house this time of year?"

"Sure, but he damn sure never did."

"Mine neither. Well—" He threw his leg over the saddle and checked the mule. "He's coming to Johnny Yellowtail's tonight."

"I thought—"

Prie rode over and stuck a cigar in Nate's mouth. "Quit thinking. It's almost Christmas."

Nate looked back and, at last, turned to the front as they rode away from the dugout "Well, he damned sure won't forget this one, I'm here to tell you."

"That's what I've planned." Prie smiled and sent the mule off in a jog trot for the ferry.

A PRAIRIE
BRIDE

FOR THREE, OR MAYBE FOUR, months in the saddle and the bawl of cattle in your ears going north to get there, drovers pushed the herds to the railheads. Two thousand head of cattle make that very harsh bawl when they stampeded. Hooves thundering on the prairie in lightning flashing thunderstorms were nights of hell in chasing cattle to get them to turn and stop them. Being the boss—that was the hard part of these drives.

He dropped off the rise and saw a soddy and a fenced garden beside it. Smoke rose out of the chimney from a cooking fire. A young woman came to the door. She looked tired, and he wondered if she had children. Then he noticed three fresh small graves beside her garden fence.

Dismounted, he took off his hat for her. "My name is Lang Holder. I'm in charge of that north bound herd a little bit west of here. I took a ride out to see the country. You have a nice house.

"Sit down on the bench. I'm glad to talk to you. I haven't seen another human in four weeks." She took a seat beside him with her hands beside her legs under the wash-worn dress. The look on her face said she was mesmerized, looking hard at his horse grazing through the bits and the rolling grass country like he wasn't even there beside her.

"Did your children die of something?"

Two wooden nods were all she did. "I tried to die, but it didn't kill me."

"What did you have?"

She shook her head. "They were bad sick, and nothing helped them. I had some medicine that cured things. Didn't work. I was worried. I was real sick. Had a bad fever. The little one, Janet, died first. Sam went next. Then my five-year-old boy, Ted, slipped away. Took me two days to dig their graves. I'm getting better, but I don't know why."

"God intended for you to live."

She turned and frowned at his comment. "What for?"

"To continue. Where is your man?"

Tears streamed down her face, and she sobbed. "He's dead too."

"How long ago?"

"The last man came to see me was a man he worked for. He told me that Paul died of a disease he explained sounded like our later one. Paid me a little money. Said it was all he had and left me some food. Three days later the children were down sick."

"That's terrible. You think he brought the disease?"

"I don't know. My kids started getting sick three days after he left." She rocked on the bench on her hands and shook her head.

"What is your name?"

"Kendra Stone, Mister Holder."

"You can call me Lang."

"You have a wife?"

"No. My fiancée died two years ago in a buggy accident weeks before our wedding.

She reached over and clutched the top of his hand. "That was terrible."

"I wondered why I wasn't with her and killed too."

She nodded.

"What will you do?"

"What can I do?"

"Start life over."

She nodded numb like but never looked up.

Then she wet her lips. "I'm sitting here in rags. I need a sponge bath, my hair washed, and to clear my head. You don't have a wife, so I won't be hurting your marriage or reputation if you would please a desperate woman."

"What is that?"

"My husband has been away from me for months working on a job before he died. I am a woman. Dirty and I know not too neat, but if you forgive my boldness, could I be your bride today?"

"Kendra, would that help you?"

"I think it would. Would you wait for me to do that? Cleanup, I mean."

"I could do it with you if you would let me and be honored."

Her blue eyes looked into his face. "That would not turn you away."

"No. We could do it together, and I won't embarrass you."

"I need to heat some water."

The water heated, and she undressed in the shadowy house. "You aren't embarrassed to see me naked?'

"No, you look like an angel."

"Hardly an angel."

"You want to back out?"

"No, I would rather kiss you." Her shoulders slumped down. She shook her head at him.

They kissed, and he held her bare shoulders. "Get your shoulders back. I think you once were a proud girl. Become one again."

"It will be hard."

"No, it will help your spirits."

She straightened her shoulders, and he smiled.

When the water was hot, he washed her back and then rinsed it. Her arms next, and she did her under arms. When she started to do her breasts, he took the rag away, sat on the chair facing her, and washed them with care. Her shoulders were back, and she made a beautiful picture as he gently moved the rag over her. She pulled back, and he found the small stretch scars from her pregnancies. When he finished, she stood, and he continued. He noticed the change in her stance. This was no longer the haggard woman who met him at the door. She had a new look, and he liked it.

They washed her hair in yucca soap and worked to scrub it clean, then rinsed it with rainwater from a barrel. They dried it with flour sack towels, and then they kissed some more. She sat on his legs at ease. They took turns at brushing her hair and exchanging soft kisses with each other.

"I don't know how to tell you, but you have kissed me more than he ever did in six years."

"Really?" He could hardly believe her words.

She leaned her face on his shoulders. "He never was mean or cross with me. He just wasn't a kisser."

"Now we are close to finishing the first part, do you have any doubts about the rest of our deal?"

"No. I think your kindness toward me has me subdued." Time to kiss again.

"If we have a nice time, and we agree, I want you to go home to Texas with me and become my wife at the first preacher we can find."

She looked pained at him. "I am certain you could find and marry a virgin bride?"

"I repeat. If you like the affair we have today, then wait for me. I will be back in two months from Abilene, and we'll go to Texas. We'll get married."

She began to unbutton his shirt. He kissed her.

"Don't say no more, or I'll cry."

He took the shirt off over his head and twisted to put it on her table.

"I will get off you to take the gun belt off."

He rose, undid it and hoped she didn't see his hands shake when he hung it on a chair. While he stood, she undid his belt and then his fly.

She pulled on the sides of his legs, and his trousers fell to his knees.

"You made it hard to get my boots off."

"I'm sorry." She bent down and pulled the first one off, then the other and smiled standing before him, drawing off his pants.

He swept her up and took her to the bed.

"Let me down. I have a new sheet from my wedding I have never used." She kissed him and whispered, "Thanks."

He closed his eyes. Why did she worry so much about that? She broke away and ran to a trunk. Holding it up, she said, "Jerk that sheet off."

He did, and she whipped out the fresh sheet, and he helped her. They met in the middle and crashed into one another. They kissed and aligned their bodies and soon were man and woman.

When it was over, the silence was long. He knew he must tell her.

"I want you to wait for me. I will be back here in two months, and our honeymoon will really begin."

They kissed, and he couldn't get enough of her mouth. Finally, they parted, and she ran to relieve herself.

"I'll wait forever for you. I'm a mess, and I know you must get back to your herd." Her knee on the bed, she chewed on her lip.

He waded across the cob mattress back to her.

"I don't know, but I think I can, or I'll try."

"Oh, Lang, if you will have me, I will sure be your bride." He fell to kissing her, and she hugged his head.

"I hope," she said using her fingers to comb her hair from her face. "I didn't shock you, but you bring out a little devil in me."

"Keep him. I wouldn't have it any other way. Kendra, we will have the best life that you can imagine when we get home."

"I will be clean and ready when you return."

"It will be hard to part with you."

"Whatever you like. We can do it any way you want."

"I have fifty dollars for you. That should buy you a wedding dress and food while I'm gone. Be very careful. I'll hurry back here once my business is done."

"Where do you live in Texas?"

"Kerrville. We will buy a ranch near there."

He dressed and kissed her goodbye. Putting the money in her hand, he went for his horse. On the rise, he waved to her, then swung the horse around and raced away.

BACK AT THE CHUCKWAGON AN hour later, he sat on a bench eating his evening meal after the men were through.

"You find anything today?"

"Yes," he said between bites. "I found my wife."

The crusty old man who served as cookie cleared his throat. "Where is she?'

"She's fine over in her soddy."

"You can't leave her out there. There are Indians, hard cases, and rapists running all over this prairie. Go back and get her. I can clean up this male bunch, and I'll make 'em piss farther away. They're just bashful boys that will honor her."

"Jake—I—"

"Saddle a horse for her first light and bring her back. We won't go over fifteen miles—more like twelve. We have a tent she can use."

"I guess so. We can get her things coming back. I'd die if anyone hurt her while I was gone."

"Do it first thing."

"I will. I will."

IN THE MORNING, HE PICKED a small tame horse out of the remuda. Jake found him a small saddle in the chuck wagon and two tow sacks for her things.

He used a big stout bay horse called Shivers and leading Shorty, he set out for her place. Meadowlarks rushed along his way. Some prairie chickens flushed, and a red tail hawk scolded him for invading their land. He topped the rise, and he saw her rush out the door and shade her eyes with her hands.

He dismounted on the fly and ran to hug her. He whirled her around in a circle. "I changed my mind. I'm taking you along. I can't worry about you for two months. We can get some things now and the rest when we come back."

She jumped up and down and kissed him. "Oh, Lang. I'm so excited."

He swept her up in his arms and carried her into the house. He stopped at the bed in the middle of the room. "We better be sure this is going to work."

"I think we better." She closed her hands on his face.

THEY DROVE THE CATTLE TO Abilene and sold them. They did well, and he sent his money back to San Antonio by Wells Fargo. He bought a buckboard, and they went back to her place and loaded all her things in the chuck wagon.

At that point he told the hands going home to not run the horses and Jake's mules to death. He'd see them in Kerrville at his father's place and square up with them there . He and Kendra were going to get married at Fort Worth, and they'd be along.

She stood on her toes and kissed each one of his crew on the cheek and thanked them. They blushed and thanked her, wishing her and him well."

They took off in their buggy, and she squeezed his leg. "I am glad we are getting there in two weeks."

"Why is that?"

"You know the first time we made love."

"I won't ever forget it."

"Well, I guess I was open."

He knew the term—she meant he had gotten her pregnant that night. "Damn, girl, that's all right."

She hugged his arm. "As I recall, it was like fourth of July fireworks."

"It was. It sure was fine."

"Oh, it was glorious. And it's been that way every night we've been together."

"Wait till we get married. We may break down the bed."

"I'm ready, cowboy, but I may faint if it gets any better."

"I can't wait."

She reached over and kissed him.

———————

THEY HAD SIX CHILDREN, AND both lived to be ninety. Together they built a big Texas ranch kingdom, and folks still talk about the dedication they had for each other. Family members, who tried to trace her ancestry, never got beyond her wedding to Logan Stone in Missouri at age twenty. He was twenty-four. Her maiden name was never listed.

THE NO NAME LADY

LADY

THINGS WERE IN A HELLACIOUS uproar across southeast Arizona and southwest New Mexico. The U.S. Army Cavalry and Army Scouts had been charging all over the area after renegade Apache. Most folks had brought their families into the small towns from their ranches in the area under the threat of more Apache attacks. While others set up fortifications at their home ranches and were armed to the teeth to withstand any attacks.

Burt Waller had gone into Tombstone for supplies and was headed back to his ranch with a swift team of horses hitched to his buckboard. No grass was growing under those ponies' hooves when he reached a corner in the trail and about ran over a prone body in the road. His quick actions avoided hitting the body on the ground, and he stood up and hauled the lathered team to a stop.

Who was in the road? He wrapped up his reins, drew his Colt .44, just in case, and jumped down to see if they were even alive. He found the person was wrapped in a blanket and when he turned her over, he discovered she was a young, pale faced, unconscious woman. With the hair on the back of his neck standing up, he looked over the chaparral country. Nothing moved or showed themselves. He holstered his handgun, swept her up, and put her in the back between his supplies.

Who was she? She had no blood on her, nor did she look beat up. How did she get out there? She didn't wake up in his transfer. Maybe at Childers Crossing someone would know where she belonged. He climbed back onto the spring seat wondering who, why, and where as he slapped the horses on their butts and sent them southeast.

Occasionally, he looked back over his shoulder at her still form. There was not a sign of consciousness in her. She had been breathing and not too troubled. But whatever, he'd be at Childers's shortly and maybe someone there could answer his questions.

He topped the next hill and saw the smoke. That was something on fire. Childers had a small store and saloon at the crossroads between Tombstone and the road to Fort Huachuca. That store must be burning ahead. Damn those Indian bastards anyway. The raiders would be gone by the time he got there, and the tall streak of smoke would draw any Army outfit in the desert there immediately. He stood up, and his passenger wrapped in the blanket between his supplies had not moved. He hoped she had not died. Nothing he could do but drive on.

He took a shortcut toward his place risking running head on into a band of Apache out in the brush. The greasewood rubbed his spokes, and the smell of creosote was powerful. He crossed the sandy dry wash and could see the ranch and corrals. He swept into the yard, and the two Mexican boys, Ornaldo and Miguel, came from the house armed with Winchesters.

"Ah, you made it," Miguel said. "Who is that?"

"We better get her inside. Help me get her out. Be careful. She's unconscious. I found her lying on the road."

"Open the door," he said with her in his arms. He carried her in to put her on his bed in the middle of the room.

Her blue eyes flew open in shock. "Who are you?"

"Burl Waller. Who are you?"

"I'm sorry. I'm not sure." She looked like she was in shock about the fact that she couldn't spit out her name.

"I don't know your story lady, but you're safe here. These boys and I are armed to the teeth. This old rock house is a fort. It has a tin roof, so fire arrows won't burn it down. But we're ready. Now you rest, and your past will catch up with you."

"I am very grateful for you seeing about me. My mind is very confused." She fell back on the pillow and held the back of her hand to her forehead. "Why can't I tell you where and who I am?"

He folded his arms. "I repeat, you're safe here. Don't fret. Things will return to you. The more you worry, the more you lock them out. The boys and I aren't great cooks, but we will fix something to eat. I bet you have missed some meals."

"I don't even know that."

"Rest."

"I will try."

He turned to his two helpers. "Any Indians come around while I was in town?"

"No," Ornaldo said to him. He was eighteen and a good hand with a gun, rope, or horse.

Miguel, his shorter cousin, was sixteen and a smart youth too. Both boys had been raised in Apacheria, and they knew their threat well. They had lost family members in raids on the village where they were raised south of the U.S. border. Help was short. The high paying mines in Tombstone got the miners. Not many cowboys looking for work ventured into the region because of the Apache. So, he and his boys ran his ranch and used the good local beef market to make a profit on his operation.

They soon had some frijoles on the wood burning range to cook. He also started to boil some oatmeal, thinking it might be more kind to her stomach, plus the beans would require hours to be boiled tender.

When he glanced over at their patient, he discovered she had slipped off into sleep. Good, maybe rest would restore her mind. He hoped so. She was someone's wife, daughter, or whatever. She was nice enough looking, and her clothes were not rags and spoke of some wealth. Too nice a female anyway for a crusty thirty-two-year-old rancher who'd been a bachelor all his life like him.

He came out of Texas after the war. Found this ranch and had enough money of his own from cattle drives to Kansas to buy the Three L. He wondered, if he'd known then the full threat of the Apache, if he'd ever have bought there. But he had to make it work or turn up his toes. The beef market in Tombstone was a good one, so he stayed. This would be his third year in the territory. He bought stocker cattle in Mexico, drove them up and ranged them on his wide valley's grass until they fattened.

He and his two hands made the deal work. With his palm, he scrubbed the two weeks beard stubble on his face, something that hadn't bothered him until he got in her company. Oh, she'd soon be back where she belonged and never worry for a minute about his shaggy looks or the dusty six-foot tall cowboy that found her lying in the road.

———————

HE FELT GUILTY HAVING THIS woman on his hands with three men and her cooped up in a small jacal. She was very modest, but she didn't know her name for anything. That frustrated her, he could tell, but she never complained. Soon, she did the cooking, and they enjoyed an improved diet.

Some troopers came by to check on them and said, the Apache renegades they thought had gone back to the Sierra Madres in Mexico. They knew nothing of her or where she came from. So, he planned to take *Jane* to Tombstone in the morning. They had a nice arm's length relationship, but he never was much of a ladies' man. She acted very reserved and demure, not like some ladies of the night he occasionally spent time with in one of the sporting houses in Tombstone.

He cleaned up and put on his white shirt, tie, and coat. They let her have the casa after they brought her heated bath water. She thanked them. When she was ready, he helped her onto the buckboard seat, and they ran off to Tombstone.

His first stop was the courthouse. None of Sheriff Behan's deputies recognized her. They acted like he should leave her there with someone until her people came looking for her since she had no knowledge of who she was. That was not what he planned short of finding her people. He checked with several people and left a notice to be printed in both newspapers that a young woman had been found and due to her lack of memory needed to be identified.

When he left the last paper office, she put her hand on his knee on the buckboard and spoke quite frankly. "I am afraid someone will say that she is mine and not be telling the truth, and I'd have to go with them, Burl."

"Only answer for that is for me to buy a marriage license and marry you."

"Oh, you don't have to do that." They were stopped in his buckboard about to block traffic.

"If your real man came, I'd apologize and give you back. That way they couldn't take you like you're talking about."

"I don't want to be a burden."

"Would you marry me?"

She nodded and acted relieved.

"Good enough. Let's do it."

He turned the rig around and went back to the courthouse. Getting a marriage license for *Jane Doe* was not easy, but they got one, and they were married. He kissed the bride, and they went by the doctor's office.

Doc Farley rung out his left ear a few times with his index finger after checking her. He explained she might, slow like, regain her past memory. No doubt she had suffered a severe blow to the head and had no idea when that happened. He said she was extremely healthy, and then in a whisper, said she had been married sometime in the past he was confident.

Burl never took that note as anything but part of her past life they didn't know about. She looked at him concerned over the matter, and he dismissed it. "We don't know how that went is all I can say, Jane."

She agreed with his confidence, and they thanked the doctor and went out to the buckboard. He stopped her to talk before they got on the rig.

"Now, I am not pushing you into anything you don't want to do. We are married and legal like unless—"

Her finger on his lips silenced him. "I know what you are going to say. I have no one but you Burl. If I had someone, they surely would've come looking for me by now. I am your wife, and I want to be her."

"Girl, that solves all my problems. I am getting us a hotel room for tonight, and you will be my wife sure enough."

She stood on her toes and kissed his cheek. "You have treated me so nice. Thank you, sir."

That spot she kissed on his shaven face burned like a hot branding iron had done it. He got them a back room on the second floor of the Alhambra Hotel. A quieter place than the ones on the street side, and they had a honeymoon. He never regretted a second of it. For him it was like some religious ceremony to have a wife to love him.

He found her beauty and her pleasing ways toward him as some great gift from a generous God. Nothing he even deserved had been handed to him on a silver platter. Her flesh was soft and yielding when he carefully entered her. This was nothing like a tumble with some Mexican *puta*. He was shaking inside as he sought her easy like. Slowly she began to respond to him, and very soon, became a willing and enthusiastic participant.

Afterward, they both collapsed.

"You all right, Jane?"

She moaned, "No, you have made me more lost."

He rose up on his arms. "You all right?"

She pulled him down smiling. "I am teasing you."

"Teasing me?"

"Burl, I love you. I am teasing you. You are wonderful. I don't think I have done this before, but I love it and you. Take me to the clouds again,"

"Damn right, girl. We're going to make you a helluva wife, hang on."

From there on, they were lost in a wild ride to outer space that ended up with them in a pile, and they slept.

He never knew what a wife would be like. He soon found out. Every night she greeted him in their bed like a fresh wave. He heard about wives who had headaches. His never had one—never denied him her body, never acted less than thrilled at their loving, and he felt spoiled beyond most men rich or poor. He built her a *hacienda,* and they soon had two children. His ranching operation spread out, and in five years, he became one of the more prosperous cattlemen in southeast Arizona Territory.

Then one afternoon three men rode up the driveway on horseback. Skirt in hand Jane hurried from the porch to see what they wanted. She paused at the iron gate under the arch before she opened it. The unshaven men in their dust floured clothing were not who she had expected. Tough men with the hard eyes of wolves looked upon her like hungry *lobos*.

Her heart stopped in her chest. Why was the one in the center so familiar looking?

"Gawdamnit, Claire, ain't you going to come out and hug me, darling." He got off his horse and about caught his boot in his stirrup. The horse shied from him. He beat it with the reins about the face and cursed more at it while it shied away from him.

"Ain't you glad to see me, Claire?" He still fought with the panicked horse and at last gave up and tossed the reins to another.

His hands on his hips, he smirked at her. "I just got out of prison, baby. You remember when I broke out of that jail in Thatcher, and we came down here on our way to Mexico. He stuck a cigar in his mouth. I guess we were really drunk that day. You were sleeping in the back of the wagon when the horses ran off."

"I don't even know who you are, mister."

"Well, darling, the law got us before we got to the border, and I never could figure out where I lost you out of that damn wagon. A con told me in prison you might be right here. He said you lost your memory after falling out of a wagon. Damned if you ain't pretty as ever."

"Stay right there. I don't know you. I don't want to know you. Get on your horses and ride from here."

"Aw, Claire—I been in Yuma prison five years. You're still my wife, and, baby, I need you bad today." His hand went to his crotch to show her.

"Mister, you better mount up and ride out of here." She closed her eyes. She'd never been his wife, and she sure didn't know him.

"Cover me, boys—"

Burl arrived, stepped into the archway, and gently moved her over. "Let me handle them."

"I don't know them. I swear," she said getting aside.

"Who in the hell are you?" The felon went for his gun. His years in prison must have slowed his draw because the Colt in Burl's hand struck him twice in the chest. Then two rifles barked. The two others were pitched off their horses by his men's shots from positions behind the wall.

Jane sat on the ground sobbing. Burl holstered his gun and told the boys to go see about them. Kneeling down, he raised her wet face and kissed her softly on the lips.

"I heard him, Jane. Your bad dream is finally over—"

Another gunshot cut off his words, and another intruder was for sure dead.

"Jane, come get up. This nightmare is finally over. We heard what happened." He pulled her to her feet and comforted her.

"He was familiar, but I still don't recall him." They squeezed each other.

"Who in the hell wanted to remember him?" he asked her.

She smiled at him like she did that first day in their bed in Tombstone "Thank God for you and them boys being here today. I won't ever again worry about them coming back or any part of my past life. I have you, and that is all that is important to me."

Neither did it bother Burl that it was over either.

WASN'T LOOKING TO BUY THE TOWN

Reprint Tahlequah Writers

THAT HOT AFTERNOON, REAGAN HAROLD sat down his worn-out cowpony and packhorse in the dusty west Kansas town of Kurtsville to observe it all. The typical crossroads settlement out on the grassy rolling country boasted a few false front stores. It offered two saloons, a doctor, a bank, livery/freight office, a mercantile, a harness/saddle repair shop, a gunsmith, a dress and hat shop, a newspaper, and a house of ill repute above the Irish Saloon. There were a few houses scattered around and some shacks about, plus an adobe jail. Not many adobe structures that far north that he could recall but there was a saloon up at Fort Laramie made out of it. Not enough trees around these parts. Folks used what was at hand and cheap especially since a jail was at public expense.

He moved his horse and the packhorse to the livery. If the price wasn't too high, he planned to stable them. When he dropped off the saddle a whiskered man came out and spoke to him.

"You spending the night or buying the town?"

"Pard, I am staying the night. When will the railroad get here?"

"Huh?"

"When are they building a railroad though this town?"

"I never even heard of such plans."

"Well, I won't buy the place then." He threw the stirrup up on the seat and went to jerking out the sweat soaked latigoes on the girth. "How much does a one-night stay for my ponies cost?"

"Two bits apiece. A dollar if I rub them down and feed them some grain."

"Is my junk safe to leave here over night?"

"Safe as Wells Fargo. Where you headed?"

"San Antonio, I hope. I spent my last cold winter in the ice and snow."

"Easy enough to get there if you got the ass that will stay in the saddle that long."

"You give free philosophy lessons too?"

Obviously, the man did not know the word and Reagan's mouth kept getting drier. "I'll take the dollar deal."

"I'll unload 'em, feed 'em, and rub 'em down."

"I will see you in the morning."

"There's free bunks for customers back there." The old man gave a head toss down the shadowy alleyway.

"I'll probably use it—later."

He hitched up his gun belt and pants out of habit. There was no gun law sign posted at the outside coming down the road out of Nebraska. So, he made no move to disarm. The Irish Saloon's bat wing doors were well oiled. He pushed them open for a breath of sourness and cigar stink that reminded him of a thousand more such dens.

Three card players looked up under the candlelight wagon wheel. A white-aproned bartender nodded hello and welcomed him to Kurtsville with a what'll it be stranger?

"Cold beer?" he asked, satisfied the gamblers and the barkeep were near the sum of population in the place.

"Yeah."

"A big mug of your best."

"Aye, and I got you one coming. Guess you're passing through?"

"The old man at the livery acted like the whole place was for sale."

"Thurman. That's his name. He may be branching out in real estate sales. That'll be fifteen cents."

Reagan put two quarters on the bar. "I'll drink more later. That a friendly card game?"

"They'll let you play."

The beer was not cold but cool at least. What more could he expect in this God forsaken place in late summer? Montana they always had ice, Nebraska some, Kansas by this time most of it had melted.

"May I join you?" he asked with his mug in hand.

The bald-headed man looked up and blinked his eyes. "You must be a drover from the cut of your clothes?"

"Reagan's my name."

"Have a seat, Ranken."

"Charlie, his name is Reagan," the mustached man on Charlie's right corrected him.

"Excuse me, sir. He's Carp, and the one on my left is Ben. Draw poker, ante a quarter. Five card draw."

From his front pocket, he drew out some crumbled small bills and more change to put on the felt spot. He anted the quarter, and they nodded. Charlie dealt the hand. He planned to keep a jack and queen, then draw three cards. Carp bid a quarter, and he stayed. Ben raised it a quarter, and they drew cards. He had a pair of jacks, bet a quarter, and the others folded. No get rich game. He tossed in his cards and raked in the small pot.

"Is there a cafe in town?" he asked about even on his money a few hours later. He'd won a few and lost some too.

"Yeah, it's behind here in that weathered looking building. She serves good food, and she washes all her dishes in hot soapy water and rinses them. Laura Glenn is her name," Carp informed him.

"You never told us where you're headed, Reagan?"

"San Antonio. Spent my last winter in the snow."

"Be nice if you like brown skin women," Charlie said.

"Pard, I like them all."

The gamblers laughed.

"You from that country?"

"I've been everywhere from the Rio Bravo to the Canadian Rockies."

"You have a calloused ass then," Carp teased.

He agreed. His belly was telling him he needed some grub. "She have food all day long?"

"Or she'll fix it for you. Good gal."

He thanked them, and left the nickel tip out of his fifty cents to Earl on bar bill. He reset his felt hat, hitched his pants and gun belt up, and then struck out for the faded gray building. He crossed the porch and could smell the cooking. A homey aroma of something good, and the woman behind the counter was a good size woman, not fat but full figured and forty.

"Howdy. Welcome to my place. What can I do for you?"

"I been greeted friendly everywhere I go in this town."

"We are all friendly with God fearing people. The bad guys ain't that way."

"You get bad guys out here?"

She stood above him. "We get our share. Law is far apart, and they roam around looking for victims all the time. But folks like you passing through are no harm and may leave fifty cents behind."

"What do you have that is easy?"

"Sliced fresh bread?"

"Butter and jelly?" He nodded.

"Sure, and some beef cooked slow with carrots and potatoes."

"Yes, they told me over at the Irish that you were the best in town."

"Ha, they will expect a special price at breakfast."

"I guess you have regular customers?"

"Keeps my doors open. Cowboys come once a month and sometimes twice. They've eat enough beans as chuck they say they could out blow the north wind."

"Or play Yankee Doddle on their back side bugle?"

She laughed. "That is funny. You must have been there."

He watched her move off to get his food. There'd be lots of blank places south of there but few he'd find this friendly. A place you'd like to remain—it snowed there too. Come morning he'd be headed south. The tambourines and guitars called him and those *señoritas* shaking their backsides dancing and clapping castanets told him Bexar County, Texas, was where he was headed.

The meal was good as he expected. He planned to turn in early and get underway again before the sunrise—Texas was calling him.

After the meal, he found his bedroll and decided to sleep beyond the Livery under the roof of a porch on an empty shack. No bed bugs there he figured.

The sun went down, and he closed his eyes lying on top of the bedroll. His deal was made with the horse hustler to saddle and load his ponies before dawn.

From somewhere in the depth of his sleep, two women talking in the night awoke him. His fist closed on the hickory handle of his .45.

What were they saying?

"He's sleeping out here somewhere."

"Who do you need?" he asked sitting up.

"Oh!" Both jumped back and hugged each other.

"Sir, I am Laura. This is Katrina. I fed you supper," she spoke in a stage whisper.

"Yes. A nice meal."

"Katrina needs to get out of here. She has a horse. But she needs some help to get away. I told her you might help her."

"She dodging the law?"

"No. No. A man thinks he owns her, and he's a big man in places. She needs a way out of here."

"Will he send his men after her?"

Laura hesitated. "We don't know. He left on a trip today, and she ran away."

"Is that his horse she stole?"

"Is it?"

The smaller woman he could hardly make out in the starlight, spoke in a low voice, "It is his horse, yes."

"Then she will be sought as a horse thief. We will need a new outfit and leave that one here. You got any money?" He was up facing the other way and redoing his shirttail and re-buttoning his pants. Then he strapped on his six-gun and swept up his hat.

"She hasn't. I have some."

"The old man can sell her one and a saddle. Then they will have no grounds for arresting her."

"I understand."

"When will they know she is missing?"

The girl said, "When the sun comes up."

"We better get busy. I'll go wake him, but don't turn on any lights or draw any attention." He rolled up his bedroll. "And we'll get the hell gone."

"You are an angel," Laura said. "She needs out of here. She can tell you all about it later. She's like a daughter to me, you know."

The hostler found her a gentle enough sound horse after they swore him to secrecy. A saddle that she could ride on, and they loaded his packsaddle and panniers on the bay horse and saddled his dun. In the middle of the aisle with a small candle lamp Laura hugged him and her too.

"God be with you two. Be careful. And Reagan, I owe you a lot."

"We ain't got away yet."

They swept southward in the coolest part of the day ahead. The stars shone bright, and they loped easy making as little tracks as he could on the wagon road and not to stumble in the darkness. So, when daylight crept up, they were ten to fifteen miles away from the town.

The girl wore a felt hat with a rawhide chinstrap in case the wind swept it off. A proverbial south wind would rise all day in their faces until, by afternoon, it would be a threat.

They watered their horses in a small stream and remounted again to start the push to move on. He decided she must be eighteen or nineteen, slender made. Her dark hair was shoulder length, and she brushed it often while riding.

When they dropped into a walk the next time, he rode in beside her.

"Tell me the particulars of this deal?"

"Scott Walker owns the Three W ranch. I met him at some horse races. He told me he was single, and I believed him. He took me to one of his outlying ranches out here and said he'd marry me when he found time, but he had lots of business to handle.

"I was dumb and accepted it all. But I learned after a few months that he had a wife and bigger ranch. I was one of his women who he used when convenient and there was no leaving, or they'd drag you back and chain you up like you were a slave.

"I had all I could stand of him. They were off at roundup, and I'd never threatened to leave, so they thought I was content. I saddled that horse and rode to see if Laura could help me get away. She thought you might do that—and, Reagan, I appreciate so much what you're doing for me. While I can't pay you now, I will pay you back for all of this."

"Fine. We just need to be on the move headed south all the time."

"I will do my best to do that, so I can get away from him holding me in that bondage."

"You have people?"

"Yes, but I am certain by now they have written me off as a wanton woman."

He shook his head. There was no answer to that. No bridge back in most cases. Most families shunned such victims as no longer their family members. A dark hole for a woman to reach out from for help and forced them to accept a role in prostitution to survive.

First nightfall they found an abandoned homestead away from the road. They built a small fire out of dried buffalo and cow chips to heat coffee and ate jerky. He watered the horses with a pump, and they prepared to bathe in cold water in a wooden tub.

He told her she could bathe first, and he'd go off and for her to whistle when she was complete. She protested. "I am afraid. You have seen women before. Stay here."

"All right. But remember you will have to ride and live with me until we find you a safe house or place. I can't guarantee you won't arouse me."

"I will accept that as reality."

"So, you know I warned you." He had found some cedar to whittle on. To avoid spying on her he whittled and whittled. Until she was redressed and told him it was his turn.

He took a bath with no regard and knew she was close. What could he do with her? Deliver her to a convent? No. She would not get along with them. Somehow, he must haul her to safety, and only God knew where that place was.

A week on the road, they'd covered miles of endless grassland, and he wondered if there was going to be any pursuit. They were in the Oklahoma Territory portion of land close to the Texas panhandle he figured. His packhorse became a little lame. They stopped at a small rancher's outfit, and he swapped for another unshod horse for ten bucks. He borrowed a horse shooing rasp and trimmed his hard striped hooves down to a clean edge and not very deep.

The man casually asked, was she his wife?

Reagan shook his head. "Just someone I met needed moved."

The rancher accepted that and gave her another glance with a *I'd like to have her* look and went on. So did the pair. The ex-packhorse whinnied to his departing companions.

"You are set on San Antonio?" she asked one day when they stopped to water the horses.

"That's my plans. You got any?"

"Anywhere, just so that damn Scott Walker can't use my body ever again."

He didn't comment. He knew she hated Walker, but now, he knew how deep it went. Without a word he mounted up for the thousandth time, and they rode on.

They crossed the Red River on a ferry, and when they were in Texas over on the high ground, he reined up and looked back at the crossing where they came from in the big cottonwood trees beside the stump choked river.

"You ever use this crossing going north?" she asked.

"Many a time sister. I had big red roan ox with a bell, and he'd lead them across there swimming his heart out and shake water off him on that far bank and trudge on to market."

"Lots of memories, huh?"

"You thought about a place to stake you out a spot?"

"You want rid of your extra baggage?"

"I wouldn't call you that. You ain't been no trouble. You never nagged me. I couldn't believe you were a woman and not doing that. You told me you only had one thing you never wanted to happen to you again—that never came about on my watch."

"That I am grateful for, too. How old are you?"

"Old enough to know better is all."

"How many years since you were born?"

"How old you think I am?"

"Thirty-five."

"Close. Why?"

"You're set to live in San Antonio?"

"In that country anyway. What in the hell are you getting at?"

"Well, what'cha going to do for a living?"

"Trade cattle. Whatever I can get along on."

"How big of a place would you need?"

"Hell, I don't know."

"What would a place up there around Kerrville and Mason cost?"

"Oh, a good one maybe four to six thousand."

"You need a partner?"

"I hadn't planned on taking one." His horse stomped his hoof, impatient to go on.

"You got the money to buy one?"

"I got a portion of it. Why?"

"I've got a portion of it too."

"Where?"

"You ain't ever hugged me, have you?" She started out of the saddle.

He frowned and dismounted, swinging his horse around to catch her. He barely held her in his arms, and he felt the thick money belt around her waist. But he saw her mouth calling on him to kiss her. He hadn't had that calling since he was a boy growing up south of there.

"You steal that money?"

"He owed me that money for stealing my innocence. I replaced his money belt one night with another one when he was asleep. He ain't needed any money, so he has not opened his twin to it I'd bet. Probably why he didn't send anyone after me, and he may never figure out which one of his many women traded him belts."

"You want to partner on a place?"

Her blues eyes twinkled, and she nodded big as all get out, then she squeezed his face and kissed him until he was dizzy. "You are a great guy. Yes, I want to partner on a ranch. You pick it. I'd like a river on it to wade in some time."

"Be nice. Let's find a land agent and look at some places."

Lester Hale was the man recommended to him. Lester had a two-seat buggy and the three looked for days up and down hills and forded shallow creeks. One sunny day when they were farther north than before he showed them a fancy secluded place.

The house had open, rough, hand-hewn beams, and limestone rock construction under pecan trees, a section of mostly rolling grass, and the Guadalupe River. Completely furnished in Texas ranch style. But it cost ten thousand dollars.

He knew she was excited. They had a private meeting while Lester stayed up by the house with the Mexican caretaker.

"Damn, Reagan, this needs to be our place."

"We won't have money to stock it or buy cattle if we pay that much."

"How many fool people have the cash to buy a ranch?"

"I don't know?"

"Not many. Not in Texas either. Make Lester offer them eight thousand cash."

They told Lester their offer. He shook his head. "That lawyer in San Antonio won't accept that for the estate."

"Ask him?" she insisted.

"It won't work."

"Lester, it may be a nice place for a cow buyer, but it is too far from town to live up here and them work in San Antonio."

He agreed. Lester made the offer, and four days later, the agent drove the buggy at breakneck speed out to the place they had rented.

"You did it," he shouted driving up, and the afternoon thundershower christened them in large cold drops before they got under the canvas cover hung up on trees.

They bought the place and moved their things up there.

They stood looking down the grassy bottom at the silver river shimmering in the sun that first day from the stone laid front porch.

"I ain't upset. But so far, all we've ever done is kiss?" she said kind of defiant sounding.

"Way you talked about Scott Walker, I kind of thought you were opposed to much more."

She punched him in the belly. "I never said that about you."

Then she hugged and kissed him. And later, in their new bed they consummated their partnership. He asked her to marry him, and she agreed—conditional to when the time was right.

He got busy trading cattle. Hired two cowboys and three Mexican men to garden, fix fence, mow, and farm some. Stocked the place with cows and calves. And gave the men notice there might be some bad men come by one day and to keep some loaded firearms right handy at all times—just in case.

The day it happened, he was at his desk. He was writing to a man in Fort Worth about some Shorthorn bulls he had a chance to buy from a man when he heard her say. "Oh my God, Reagan, he's here."

He took the short-barreled Colt out of the desk drawer. Who was there?

Holding the gun against his leg, he about ran into her face first in the hallway. "Who is here?"

"Look out the front door. It is him on a horse."

When he got to the open door, he saw this big smug guy sitting cross-armed on the big fancy horse. Like him to ride a hot-blooded stallion to show off.

"You're trespassing on my ranch."

"I figure it was my money bought it that that bitch stole from me."

"No, she's my wife now. I can settle anything you want from her."

"Mister, she ever wants to see you again, tell her to get her ass out here."

"Stay there." I said over my shoulder to her.

"You ain't listening to me."

"No, I'm not because my men have you and your men covered with two rifles and three shotguns. Drop your guns real slow."

"Bullshit."

I guess them were Walker's final words. I shot him twice in the chest. The stallion reared up, and he pulled him over backward on top of him. I think when his head hit the rock it finished him off. But the other four of his men lay dying or dead in the entanglement of bodies stomped on by their own frightened mounts. The gun smoke slow like drifted away.

My men nodded.

"Now, we need them buried. Sorry about that."

A deputy came out a week later and asked if we had seen a guy called Scott Walker or any of his men around there. The man was missing. Someone'd found his stallion bridle-less and a blood-soaked saddle west of Kerrville and no sign of him. A very long way from our location, how could he have gotten there from here?

He told the deputy he hadn't been there. He rode on. All Reagan's men nodded and went back to work.

It was a year later, she found they were going to have a kid, and so they got married.

The newspaper accounts had said when Walker disappeared he more than likely had thousands in cash on him that day he vanished and was probably robbed. The account made no exaggeration about that either. In fact, it was a lower amount than actually was strapped on his corpse.

Kristine sent for Laura before their first boy was born. Told her she had a better job for her in Texas than running that café. She helped run the house and played grandmother. They were no kin, but they were bonded as family.

Oh, that money he brought to them. Why that funded two more large ranches for their boys when they got big enough to handle them.

His wife said she had worried a lot before they celebrated together their first good deal. She said he never paid her any attention until that time.

He said, "Honey, I didn't figure you'd liked doing it after the bad way you talked about him."

He got punched for that too.

A
MAIN EVENT

THEY BROUGHT TWO OF THEM Larson boys in all shot up in a farm wagon. Stella Larson drove it standing behind the spring seat to Doc Harris's house, and those bay horses were sure lathered up. She must've run them ponies all the way to Luperville. Stella was a tough lady. Once, she horsewhipped a man who accused her of stealing one of his horses. It turned out later the horse was found. But when they asked him if he'd go back and apologize, he shook his head. "Not no, but hell no. That woman's a bulldog."

"Where in the hell is that damn sheriff?" She bailed out of the wagon with a shout and a show of her petticoats in the leap. "Handle them boys of mine easy."

"Who done this Stella?"

"That bunch of pig farmers. The Kanes." Her blue eyes looked black, and she cut around like she was still looking for a lawman.

"What happened?" someone asked.

"That whole Kane family came over armed to the teeth and started shooting. Said we'd ate one of their calves."

"Did you eat one?"

"Hell, no." Hands on her hips, if looks could kill—all those Kanes would have been dead. Then she hurried into Doc Harris's house after the second stretcher.

"Doc," she shouted. "Arnold is the worst shot up. Kenny is wounded but not as serious."

Doc was already standing over one of them on the operating table. Three of the other Larson family were there. They'd ridden in with her. Teal Thompson, her brother-in-law in his thirties, Nickels, her youngest son, and her sister's boy, Clete Thompson.

She went out on the porch in the growing darkness. "Someone send for the sheriff?"

"We did," one of the curious bystanders said.

"Wonder where he is?" She had her hands on her hips again. Aside from being somewhat overbearing, she was not an unattractive widow woman. She had her first son at age fourteen. He was born on the trip when her late husband hauled her, four Texas cowboys, and a few hundred longhorn cows to Arizona from Texas. Nathan Larson was twice her age and had died about five years earlier from gunshot wounds fighting Mexican bandits at their ranch in the southern Arizona Territory.

Her tall willowy frame, straight back and braided blonde hair piled on her head would have been attractive. But a coiled-up diamondback rattler looked polished too, and they'd kill you.

My name's Colby Singleton, and I've got a ranch south of town. I figured she'd give the lawman a piece of her mind for not being there at her beck and call. But I could tell her Drew Rounds was not easily shaken by much of anything, except he hated law breakers, rustlers, back shooters, and had little patience with drunks.

――――――――

THE SHERIFF, DREW ROUNDS, SAT in the captain's chair with two kings in his poker hand. He waited for someone to raise him in the cloud of cigar smoke that ringed the large table and other card players. Overhead, the candles flickered, and he felt good enough. He had won about thirty dollars so far that evening. The Panther Saloon had the usual weeknight crowd. The saloon girls were lounging around. Their business was slow that evening.

Drew paid Kathryn fifty cents to play some songs on the tinny piano. She was taking a break. A big buxom blonde from the North Country, she had an accent that was not from the south. But she could really play the ivory keys and sang about halfway good enough to listen to.

The last player folded. Drew threw his cards in face down—none of their damn business. He could have had a royal flush for all they knew. Then he raked in the pot.

Someone busted in the batwing doors. "Sheriff, Sheriff. They shot up Stella Larson's boys. She's got them over at the Doc's and wants you over there right now."

"I guess she can want me all she wants. It's too dark outside to go looking for shooters. Tell her to check with me in the morning."

"I ain't telling that woman anything."

"Wise decision." He tossed in his two-bit ante and laughed.

"What was the shooting about?" he asked the message bearer.

"She said the Kane's were mad 'cause she ate a calf of theirs."

He looked at his new cards. Nothing. "Well, I'm going to fold. Better go see what the lady needs."

"You know, Drew," Charlie Hackett said. "I'd take that hellion to bed if I could gag her. She ain't half bad to look at. But damn that mouth of hers needs a rag stuffed in it most times."

Drew nodded. "Aw, she's just worried people won't take her serious and run over her if she ain't even halfway tough as she appears."

"Half tough? Drew, we ain't talking about the same female."

"Oh, Charlie, we're talking about the same one. I better go see what I can do."

"She may kick your ass."

"She won't get a virgin at that."

They laughed, and he pocketed all his winnings. Then he gave them a salute.

The summer night was warm. Stars really sparkled, and he could see the mountain's shape in the moonlight. He neither dreaded nor feared the tall blonde, just another matter to handle in his job as county sheriff. That's what they paid him for at the rate of forty a month plus expenses. He also ran the county assessor's office and got ten percent of the county taxes collected for doing that. Unlike most territory sheriffs, he didn't use his deputies paid by the county to do law enforcement. He had an office and five people hired to do that. He spent money on the cost of doing business that few others did, however he made fifteen hundred the year before over his expenses.

Another good year and he'd have enough money to buy a well-watered ranch. That was his ambition, and he was growing lots closer to doing that. Arizona Territory had treated him well. He only had received two bullets since being elected, both of course proved non-fatal. Both shooters were planted in the ground.

When he approached Doc's lighted house, there was a crowd still in the yard. Sitting on the porch's edge looking haggard for her was Stella. She stood up and reset the waist on her dress.

"About time you got here."

"My dear, I have been coming since I heard your request." He put his arm on her shoulder and guided her inside the brightly lit room. "Tell me what's happened?"

"Those damn Kanes—"

He leaned his head in closer. He knew his arm made her uncomfortable, but he had her restrained.

"I'm sorry, Drew," she had lowered her voice. "Two of my boys are shot up. I never ate their calf. It made me so mad. I'd strangle the whole lot of them."

"I understand. Now who shot first?"

"I shot over their heads with a shotgun."

"Now, you shot first. Stella, what did you expect them to do?"

She straightened like she wanted him to take his arm off her shoulder. But he acted like it should be there and wanted to confide in her in close contact.

"Maybe it was wrong—to shoot, but they made me so mad accusing me— you know what I mean?"

"I do, but if your life isn't in danger, don't shoot at people. They shoot back."

In his soft voice intended for her alone, he said, "Now a jury is going to say, she shot first. Them Kanes had to fire back."

"I don't—" she lowered her voice. "Drew what could I do?" Her eyes were wet with tears. "I hope my boys don't die."

"What's doc said?"

"Oh, they'd probably make it."

"That's good. Now, I bet we can go in the back and have some coffee. He always has coffee made when I come up here."

"Sure. I'm glad you came. I don't know why, but you remind me so much of my late husband. I could be mad enough to kick six guys asses in, and he'd say, 'Stella, rest easy.'"

"He must have been a great guy."

"He was, Drew. He really was, and I know if he'd been here, he'd have me calmed down just like you've done."

"Stella, I want you to meet me at the Cactus Ridge School house next Saturday night. They're raising money for Able Ponder's widow. What color box will you have for your supper we're going to share?"

"What makes you so all fired certain I'd meet you there?" She glanced around, trying to see if anyone in the room heard her outburst. But his arm over her shoulder restrained her from doing much more than being in their private huddle.

"'Cause it is a respectable place to court you?" His finger on her lips silenced her having an outburst.

"Court me? Why I—"

His finger silenced her again. "I am not a bum. I have some money. I'm single. Never been married, but I want to know you lots more. Now, before you have a hissy fit, let's see how your boys are."

They both straightened. He silenced her once more. "Nothing here to get mad about. Be easy. I hope they're fine, and I bet they'll heal. Let's go drink coffee after you talk to the doc again about your boys."

A short while later, they discussed what the doctor'd said about her boys' condition and sipped the fresh coffee. Doc had to leave and deliver a baby with a woman having trouble.

"What were you doing?" she asked.

"Playing poker. And winning. You play poker?"

"You made me remember. I played poker with my husband a lot when we were first married, and I lost a lot."

He could see some amusement in her small smile at the recollection. Then she shook her head and touched her hair. "I don't know if I have my head on."

"You look very nice this evening. I'm so sorry we meet like this, under such unfortunate circumstances."

"Whatever made you think of that box supper auction?"

"You."

She actually blushed. "It will be your toes get stepped on if we dance."

"You have never danced with me."

"How old are you?"

"Thirty-two."

"You've never been married?"

"No one would have me."

"That's a lie, and I know it."

"How?"

"Anyone that can turn my fire down and me not get madder, has to be well acquainted with women."

"Did I turn your fire down?"

"Well, I am not ranting and raving at you am I?"

"No, and I appreciate that. But, Stella, you're an attractive woman. I knew if I could ever get inside the loud fence you throw up, I'd find the real lady you are."

She chuckled in her throat. "Only one man ever did that to me. God rest his soul. But I'm thinking God must have sent you—Drew, I feel silly as I was when I met him that first time in our ranch house yard."

"That sounds good. Now, I intend to settle this war between you and them."

"Pig farmers," she said under her breath.

"We all have to make a living."

She made sure they were alone in the kitchen seated at the table. "You won't change me."

"Oh, Stella, you need to be more generous to people. No one's all there. Few think as fast as you do."

"You're serious about that box dinner deal?"

"Does that worry you?"

"You? Yes."

"Why?"

"Well, I guess I'd have to think about something to wear. Do you like my hair up like this?"

"I guess I'm asking you for a secret."

"Secret? Most guys would want to know what color my box was so they'd not to have to eat with me."

"There you go. I asked for that information."

She nodded in surrender. "I am not a bit sure why you'd do that."

"Trust me."

"I guess I am going to have to. Red ribbon on it in a bow."

He finished his coffee. "Is anyone here to take you home tonight?"

"Why no. I didn't know how long I'd be. I sent them all home on the horses they brung to be sure no one burned me out."

"I'll get a horse and drive you back."

She shook her head. "I have no fears going home alone."

"I do."

"Why?"

"Do I need a reason?"

She smiled and shook her head. "Whatever does *that* mean?"

"Do I feel like you need some protection? I do."

"I've been by myself since he was killed—five years ago now."

"Time you considered it as unhealthy."

"Who *are* you?"

"A person who has an interest in your wellbeing."

"I'm a loudmouth—"

His finger on her lips silenced her. "You're a very strong woman. I like that."

"Where did you come from?

He chuckled. "Trust me. I am an admirer."

"*If* I let you see me home, what do you expect?"

"Nothing."

She shook her head and looked away.

"Stella, I'd like to convince you to trust me."

"If you want to see me home, I accept your gallant offer."

"Thank you. You need anything?"

"I hate to go that far away tonight and not get back up here in the morning to check on them two."

"It won't look very good, but you can stay at my house here in town."

She considered it. "I really don't give a damn what people think about how I run my life."

"Fine. I have a bedroom upstairs."

"That will be all right, and I can be back here then early in the morning. Thank you."

So, they had her team put up at the livery and walked under the stars two blocks to his residence.

"I suppose tongues are clacking already."

"Oh, yes, we are having such a lusty time. Stella, I don't give a damn."

"You've never had a wife?" she asked as they strolled.

"No. I was a ranger in Texas. That is not conducive to having a wife."

"My, my, you use words I have never heard before in my life."

"I'm sorry. It means there was no place for a wife. There."

"I bet that was right. You might improve my conversations if you don't get tired of me asking dumb questions."

Ahead of her he opened the yard gate and showed her the way onto the porch. He opened the door and let her inside. "I'll put on a light. Wait here."

He struck a match for the lamp on the table. Then he blew the match out and turned up the flame.

"You have a nice house."

"I have a housekeeper."

"She does a nice job." Stella was admiring things in the living room.

"Yes, I am very pleased with her."

"If I was impulsive, I'd turn out the light and hug you for being so nice to me tonight."

He spun her around and hugged her. "I don't need a lamp turned off to hug you."

She put her face on his shoulder. "It feels strange. I never imagined I would be in another man's arms ever again."

"Maybe you've missed something?"

"I believe a widow needs to honor her husband's death."

"Five years is plenty."

"You confuse me."

"No. I am who I am. You should be who you are. We are grown up people, and life is for the living."

She nodded. "I don't know—what I want to do. One says kiss him. One tells me I'm a dumb fool."

He raised her chin and kissed her.

"Thank you." She buried her face in him.

"You feel foolish?"

"No. Give me time."

"I have lots of time."

She sniffed.

He found his handkerchief. "I didn't do that to break your heart."

With care she wiped her tears. "I know."

"How hard must I work to break down your iron coat of armor?"

She shook her head. "I may be hopeless."

"The bed is upstairs on the right. The linen is fresh. You can lock the door with a bolt."

"Why would I do that?"

"To feel comfortable."

"I understand one thing, you're on a mission, and I am flattered. Kind of scared, I have scared off most men who even showed an ounce of interest in me. But you caught me tonight unaware."

"Come now." He shook his head. "In the past five years, you haven't had one man come by you, and he made you stop and measure him?"

"I don't recall one."

"Never had an affair in your married life?"

"No."

"Well, I won't hurt you."

"I never looked at another man in my life. Nathan Larson came down the road to our place buying horses in Texas when I was twelve. I married him the next year. My mother bawling her eyes out 'cause not only was he marrying me but taking me to Arizona. I never got to see her again. He was the only man in my life."

"And that was the story of your life."

"Yes, it really was."

"So, life goes on. We can talk more at the box supper."

She nodded. "In case you're keeping score. You are the number two man to ever kiss me as well."

Her words made him smile. "I called that taking liberties."

She laughed. "I called that me being off guard. I can't say I didn't like it. But you shocked me."

"I liked doing it."

"A man would wouldn't he?"

"Yes. I had an attractive woman in a situation where I could kiss her, and I liked it."

"You're a strange man, Drew Rounds."

"I'll fix breakfast about sunup."

"I don't aim to be any bother—"

"See you then."

"Thanks, anyway."

He watched her go up the stairs. "You need a light up there."

She looked back. "I can find my way."

He waited until she shut the door. Then he blew out the lamp, went to his back bedroom, undressed, and went to bed. Round one was over. It might be a full fifteen round fight to get her head turned around. But after this one, he felt he might have found her worth the whole fight. He'd see. He'd have to see how her boys got along and then go see the Kanes. Folks had to learn you reported crimes to the sheriff, not take them in your own hands. Him and his men answered questions and resolved things. They'd sent several convicted felons off to the new Territorial Prison in Yuma. But it had to be handled by the law and judges. Hard for some folks to get used to the system.

She would have been nice to share his bed with, but he had plenty of time. He rolled over and went to sleep.

Must've been the smell of his Arbuckle coffee brewing, brought her down the stairs. She hardly looked awake.

"Morning, Stella. You get any sleep?"

"Some. You look fresh." She took the steaming mug from him. "You get up like this every day?"

"Most days. I don't sleep much."

"I have to thank you. I thought about the supper auction too."

"You change your mind?"

"No, you can die from my bad cooking if you like, but I must warn you, I don't think I could have another family."

"Did I—"

"I just wanted you to know if you were stuck on having a family, I'm damn sure a poor candidate."

"Never crossed my mind. I really don't care."

"Well, I wanted you to know that."

"Good." He chuckled as he filled her plate with fried taters, sausage patties and scrambled eggs.

"What is so funny?" She was amazed looking at the platter of food. He was getting some golden-brown biscuits out of the oven and slid them on a platter.

"Come what may."

"What does that mean?"

"Eat while it's hot. Did you think that would bother me?"

"I wanted you to know the truth."

"I won't buy a baby bed then." He took a seat and broke open two steamy biscuits to butter.

"Now you're picking on me."

He rose up. "Look at me." When she did, he kissed her on the mouth and sat back down. "Now, I am the first second guy who kissed you twice."

She laughed then and shook her head. "You are a funny romantic guy."

"Keep thinking like that."

"I bet you've broken a lot of girl's hearts."

"I think that's the other way around. I came back home twice to see nice young ladies who I planned to ask them to marry me, and they'd gave up and married some other guys. Both told me they thought I'd be a ranger till they were old maids."

"How old were they?"

"Oh, sixteen or seventeen."

"Don't laugh. I thought that about him when I was twelve."

"He write you letters that year?"

"He had his sister write me letters, and she answered mine like he had written them when he was off horse trading. Oh, I thought he was the best man in the world. Some time passed while I was waiting. It was springtime. Those dang blue bonnets made spreading carpets that year, and I figured any guy that could describe them like she did was all right."

"How did you find out he never wrote them."

"Day we went to the JP to get married, and he was about to sign the marriage certificate. He elbowed me. "Read that, I don't have my glasses."

"That's how you knew?"

"Why he never had any glasses. And he explained on our honeymoon that he paid his sister fifty cents to write me every two weeks."

"I never wrote those two but maybe once a month. But I wrote them."

"You want a job?"

"Doing what?"

"Cooking breakfast. I'd hire you. Boy you really are a good cook."

"Look at me."

"No, I'm going to stand up and hug you too. It is so damn good."

That time they really kissed, and she felt wonderful in his arms. He thought she was also getting into this kissing business. Ring the bell timekeeper. He'd outscored her in round two.

"I need to get over and see about the boys when we get through—ah, kissing and eating." They sat back down.

He could have sworn she was blushing. She was awful intent on eating his food.

One more cup of coffee, and he walked her in the cool predawn to the doc's place. He went inside with her. The assistant told her both were resting, and they had no problems except getting over their wounds.

"I am going to wait around here until they wake before I go home," she said.

"I'll go see what's wrong at the office if there is anything. I'll see you Saturday night."

She checked and the assistant was gone. She walked him outside on the shadowy porch and hugged him. Dawn was only pinking the eastern sky, and they kissed.

"Thanks for all you did."

"Nothing. But we will have more time together."

She closed her eyes. "I wish those boys hadn't been shot—but they kind of brought us together."

"Yes, I had a chance to slip up on your blind side."

"Oh, go on. I saw you coming, and there was not one damn thing I could do to stop you."

"Stella, you're lovely."

"Keep that badge polished and your head down."

He waved and left her. He could've run to the office, but he'd probably have gotten tangled up in his spurs and flopped on the ground. Whew, there was lots of woman there.

SATURDAY, HE HAD SOME THINGS to resolve in his office. Two of his own men had an altercation, and he wanted it straight. He had both deputies seated in his office and sat behind his desk in the swivel back chair.

"You two get in a fight over at Kelly's Saloon last Thursday night?"

They both nodded.

"Was it over a dove works there?"

"Yes."

"Now, doves are not wives. They work for everyone, right?"

"So, neither of you has a brand on her ass, do you?" He stared at them hard.

"No, sir."

"Then make up your minds. If you are going to work for me, then you have to stop arguing over them. If you had been doing your duty, and two guys got into it over her, you'd have arrested both of them. I don't have a head count of all the ladies we have working in the two houses and the saloons in this town, plus some more working out of row houses, but surely to God one of you could find another woman."

"Yes, sir."

"I will fire you both if I hear about it again. We set examples for the citizens as lawmen. Fighting over a whore in public or in the alley is not what my deputies do."

"Yes, sir."

"I'm going to that box supper auction tonight. Both of you are on duty every Saturday night for a month. I don't expect to hear any more about fighting. Now, get the hell out of here."

They left and his chief deputy Ray Allen came in. "They tell you who she was?"

"I didn't give a damn. I told them they fought over one more, I'd fire them."

"Her name is Clair."

"Good, she can go on down the road, too, if she's involved in any more trouble."

"What did the Kanes' say about the shootout?"

"They had been mad. I told them mad or not they must come in pay a fine for their disturbing the peace and if anyone died, they'd all face manslaughter charges. And I'd jail them for six months if they didn't come to town the next time. Report the crime to us so we could handle it." I was tired of this vigilante business.

"You get your bluff in on them."

"I think so. I am going to the box supper auction."

"You got one picked out?"

"Have to see how high they will go."

"Have fun. I think we have a lead on the guy shot the cowboy over at Evens Town."

"Who's that?"

"Bradley Stovall. I'm checking up there to see if he's in Tucson."

"Handle it. I won't be back until in the morning some time."

"Have a good time."

"I'll try."

He went by the livery and took out his horse, curried him down. He looked good enough saddled to ride over there. His bedroll and hobbles tied on, he headed in that direction. Several folks would already be camped over there, so he had no worries about finding lunch.

The bay horse was a little frisky when he swung up on him. But he kept him in close check riding out of town. Traffic was beginning to pick up. Folks coming in like usual on Saturday to get supplies and other traffic, like the guy brought the mail out of Tucson in a buckboard waved. Some freighters had yoked up after camping beside the road and were ready to move on.

He arrived before noon, and after watering him, he hobbled the bay horse at some distance north of the whitewashed schoolhouse. His saddle on its horn and the bed roll with it, he hitched his six-gun and walked over to the parked chuck wagon marked with the Bar 66 brand.

Lassiter McCall was lounging in a canvas chair under a canvas fly fluttering some in the wind. The mustached rancher had a tin cup in his hand.

"Coffee or whiskey neighbor."

"Coffee's fine." He wore his metal cup on his belt and handed it to his black man, Cousey, who was McCall's cook and handyman.

"You sure you don't want none of his fine whiskey, Mister Sheriff?"

"Coffee will do. Thanks."

"How are things going?" McCall asked. "You still working on our bet?"

"No big problems. I still have six months on our bet. Ain't had a horse stolen report in two weeks."

"Hell, that's slow business then."

The black man brought his cup back steaming with coffee.

"You don't take nothing in it do you's, sah?" he asked him.

"I just drink coffee. Thanks."

"You looking for anyone up here?"

"No business today."

"Something must be up. You ain't drinking free whiskey."

"I'll be fine. How's your livestock?"

"We've got some rain along. They're doing good. Always use more."

"That's the Arizona national anthem. You know, more rain." Coffee was still too hot to sip.

"It wasn't any wetter in Texas. I'd been smart I'd have moved up in that blue stem country in Kansas. But them folks were still fighting the civil war. Me and Cousey decided it would be too damn hard to live amongst them."

"Dey sure wasn't over dee fighting back then."

"I saw that too. Shame, on those first trips to Abilene there was grass for a million cows up there."

McCall shook his head. "Honyockers came and plowed most of it up."

"Well, folks are pulling in for tonight. You got here early?"

"Some of my hands are coming this evening. Cousey is cooking some roast for us for tonight. I'm about to have him cut us off a slab. You can eat now can't you?"

Drew made a face. "I didn't come to bum a meal."

"But by Gad you'll eat some of his mesquite wood cooked prime beef."

"Yes, I will."

"Cousey, serve him some."

The white whisker-stubbled black man asked, "Will *dat* get us out of jail free?"

"Any time you need a pass, let me know."

McCall shook his head at them. "Hell, us two old farts aren't getting in jail anymore, are we?"

"No sah, we be dee over dee hill bunch." Then he laughed putting the big, browned chunk of roast on his block of wood to carve.

He cut a slab off on a plate and set it on the table. Then he did another. Juices ran out of it while his sharp knife slipped down it. Drew could imagine how mouthwatering good it would be.

Next, he had some French bread that he tore off chunks for them eat. "Now you two dig in."

"Ain't you going to eat with us?" McCall asked his man sounding disappointed.

"No siree. I don't be hungry yet."

They didn't talk much. The rich food was so damn good.

Between bites, Drew said, "I see why you came early. This is powerful good."

After he ate until he was full, thanked them, he went on and visited others. Her and a bandaged boy showed up. Drew didn't want to disrupt her visiting around the camp, so he sat back. But he got a good look at the red bow when she put it inside the schoolhouse where women were busy setting things.

The day moved fast, and soon Colonel Tom Ralston was telling everyone the auction was starting. The schoolhouse was loaded. The auctioneer and his helpers were on the stage and the bidding was good.

One of the workers brought the bidder a ticket he had to pay for before he got the box, and then he learned who he had to sit with. They picked on some, running them up so their suitor had to dig deep to eat with her. Some lost. When the worker held up Stella's box supper, the colonel asked what would they give.

"Twenty dollars," Drew said. That was twice the going price and the colonel couldn't get a rise. "It goes for a good cause. Our Sheriff bought this dinner. Give him some applause." They did.

Some smart ass asked him if he knew who's he'd brought, and Drew never answered him. The helper gave him a ticket and said, "It's for twenty dollars."

"Thank you. I can pay it."

"Yes, sir."

He stood in line, paid for the box, and started off with it. She got up and joined him. "Where are we going to eat it?"

"You pick the place."

"Over there is room." She pointed to a spot.

"Fine."

"You know you shocked some folks?"

"Not you?"

"Of course not. I never told my son, who's here either. He said, do you know the sheriff bought it?"

"Nice joke, but I am glad you could come."

"I wondered if you were even here till I saw you."

He nodded. "You had friends to meet and greet. I didn't want to be an anchor."

"That was very nice of you. I guess it was something new. I understand now, but I was afraid I'd scared you off."

"Telling me we wouldn't have children?"

She quickly nodded. "I can't help some things. I will just blurt them out."

"It was kind of you."

"No, it wasn't. It was rude. It simply was in the front of my mind. He needs to know."

"That's good. You're thinking about the two of us."

She looked up and closed her eyes. "I have not been able to think. There are so many ifs in my way. I hope you like chicken."

"I like chicken."

"You'd like anything tonight."

"Stella," he said, "we'll simply have fun here. Stop being so serious. Let your hair down."

"I'll try hard."

"Good." They ate her food, and he loved her chocolate cake. She got them lemonade to sip on.

"Here, try this." She set his cup of it down. "Missus Lemon asked me, the old biddy, if you were announcing our engagement tonight."

"Should I?"

She put her hands on him to hold him down. "I said you had not even asked me."

"Music's starting. It's a waltz." He stood up, and she did too.

They waltzed away. If there was anyone else in the schoolhouse, they didn't know, and they didn't care. They went swirling around the floor oblivious to any and all. She was so easy to turn and keep up with. He could not believe his good fortune in finding her.

She finally closed her eyes. "Am I going easy enough to suit you now."

"Perfect, my dear. You are better than any ballerina."

She frowned at him. "Where did you ever see one of those?"

"I paid well in Dodge once to see them whirl on their toes."

"I am really jealous. All I have ever seen is pictures. But I am not a ballerina."

"You are to me."

"What a weak mind you have."

"Better to love you with."

They whirled around, and she looked at the ceiling—for celestial help he decided. No matter, she was his, and he loved every moment of it. Polkas, they really went full steam and the square dances the same. They went outside in the starry warm night and in the shadows, they pressed their foreheads together.

"Where will you sleep tonight?" she asked.

"In my bedroll."

"Do you have two?"

"No, but it is big enough for two."

"Ever tried it for that many before?"

"Not in years."

She kissed him. "How many years?"

"I have forgotten."

"After tonight, I would have forgotten everything in my past also. Oh, Drew, how did this turn into such a magnetic force. Do you feel it?"

"I felt it at my house holding and kissing you."

"I felt it in that bed. Why were we sleeping apart? I never felt like that in my life except prior to my marriage to him."

"I didn't come up here to ruin your reputation. I came up here to win you over to me."

"I finally realized that. Now, I am the one wanting, and you have this cool way about you."

"I would love to hike you out there and share my bedroll with you. But I want you to be without your conscience slamming you tomorrow."

"Let me find my son, Kenny, and tell him my plans. How will I get home?"

"That bay horse rides double?'

"Good Lord. I haven't ridden double on horseback in years." She kissed him hard, then left.

He leaned back against the schoolhouse. Round three was won. Ring the bell, Judge.

She returned swishing her skirt and looked him up and down. "I found him. I told him."

"What did he say?"

"Fine. That was it."

"He really knows?"

"What we are going to do? Yes."

He fit his hand in hers, and they went across the grassy flat. The horse threw his head up and then went back to grazing. He unfurled his bedroll.

"I need to unbutton my shoes. Can I sit on top of it? I should've worn boots. I can dance in them, too, but I thought, well, it was more ladylike to wear shoes. More ladylike to sleep in your bedroll too, huh?"

He lay on his belly and chewed on a grass stem. "I'd say it was fine."

She gave him a push with her shod foot. "Oh, I have forgotten all about how men act. Of course it is fine, if they get their way with a woman."

He rolled over onto his back and stared up at the stars. "You learned at an early age."

"About what men wanted?"

"Yes."

"I was young. My mother's advice on my wedding eve was, 'Endure it darling. I have to.'"

The last shoe off, she unhitched her long silk stockings and peeled them off. Unbuttoning the front of the dress, she halted. "You haven't kissed me for a while."

"I didn't want to disturb you undressing."

She crawled over and kissed him while he lay on his back. "Then disturb me."

He did. They both were giggling, and with the dress open, he raised the slip and kissed her nipples. She shuddered and moaned.

He screwed off his boots. Raised up on his knees he unbuckled the gun belt, while she unbuttoned his shirt. Finished undressing, she slipped under the covers with him only getting a hint of her body. Pants and underwear gone, he went under the covers, too.

They lay side by side. He closed his eyes and slowly felt her hips and stomach. They kissed and kissed until she whispered. "Take me. I'm yours."

He did. They fell into a whirlpool and eventually swam out, exhausted and holding each other tight. He was not sure theirs had been a made-in-heaven affair, but it was the most exciting encounter he ever had and far exceeded any expectation he could have dreamed about achieving with her.

"You know, I could cry. Are you telling me that we could've done that in a real bed three nights ago?"

"No, the anticipation made it better for the both of us. That put a better light on a more savory conclusion out here on the prairie."

She snorted and shook her head ruefully. "Now, what in the hell did you do to me for that?"

"We made love."

"No, you were right. It was a lot more complicated than that. Now, I imagine you want to ride off into the sunset."

"Stella, I'm not leaving you. We've found each other. Haven't we?"

She pulled his face down on hers. "Oh, yes. I find it hard to believe you found all this in me."

"I think we'll have lots of fun."

"No doubt. But now that you have me, where will we live?"

"As long as I'm sheriff, I need to live close to that office."

"Those boys are finally going to have to learn how to run that ranch. When do we get married?"

"When do you want to?"

"You tell me."

"No, no. I know better than that. The woman has to set that date. My mother taught me that."

"Two weeks, then. But I want to have you between now and then. You won't be baggage to go around with me, and I won't be in your way."

"I can do that. By the way, McCall and his cook are fixing breakfast for us tomorrow morning."

"Why is that?"

"Six months ago, I told him I wanted to get involved with you. He bet me ten to a hundred I couldn't ever get to you. He'll buy your wedding dress."

"How much time did you get?"

"One year's time and six months comes soon."

"Oh, Drew, I'm the happiest woman in the world."

Why did it take so long for him to find someone? In the end he decided he probably wasn't looking for her in the first place.

A KNIGHT IN CHAPS

HEADED HOME CROSS-COUNTRY, I came off the cedar-live oak hills into the basin and found a piped spring with a cow tank made of rocks. Stepping off my jaded horse, I pulled down the tight crotch of my pants and waded over in my chaps to get a drink. Beggar was sloshing his bits in the water beside me. I was belly down on the rock wall drinking the fresh cool water when a pistol shot about made me fall in the water to get back on my feet.

There, onboard a big sorrel horse, a blonde headed girl under a flat crown expensive hat rode up and held a smoking pistol pointed at me. I looked for sight of her backup, but no one showed up. Why, she might only be eighteen or nineteen?

I picked up my hat and looked hard at her. "Lady, you just shooting for practice?"

"No, I could have shot you. This is a deeded spring, and you haven't any permission to drink from it."

"When did a man need permission to drink from a Texas stock tank?"

"Since folks started stealing Y Bar Y cattle. Now, you get up and get you and that crowbait off the property and don't come back. The likes of you aren't welcome here."

I brushed the dirt off the brim of my hat and reset it on my head. "You ever shoot at me again, little sister. I'll take that gun away from you and bust your butt."

"Listen drifter, if you don't make tracks, I'll shoot you so full of holes you'll be a sieve."

I stuck my boot in the stirrup. Then when she holstered the gun, I swung Beggar around and put spurs into him to charge her.

She went for the gun. One armed, I swept her off the saddle around the waist and reined in my horse. Her screaming bloody murder, I put her on my lap and took the gun away from her. But I was forced to drop it to fight off the hellion I'd taken. Fists hammering me in the face, on my arms, and I had to force her belly down over my lap. And then, off balanced, we landed in a pile on the ground with her on top of me. Lucky we missed any rocks, and she whipped around and demanded red face. "Just who in the hell do you think you are?"

"My name's Clint Cooper."

"Well, my name's Loretta Stone, and I am having you arrested and hung for raping me."

I began to laugh at her absurd charge.

"What do you think is so damn funny?" Her fancy hat hung on her throat on a stampede string and her blonde hair hung over half a face. That and two buttons were undone and exposed her snowy round breast tops.

"Oh," she said, slapped me like I had undone them, and then she redid the blouse buttons.

"You've been away at finishing school too long. Welcome home to Texas darling."

"My father will kill you for this."

I shook my head and put my hat back in place. The fracas had knocked it off too.

"You slap me once more. I'll give you something to slap me for."

"What is that?"

"For you to find out." I climbed to my feet and offered her a hand. She refused my offer and stood up by herself.

"Now, where has my horse gone?" She whirled around and there was no sign of him. He must have run off while I was struggling with her.

"How should I know? Was he ground tie trained?"

Her boot clad feet standing apart she ignored me opening and closing her fists like her anger was growing. Hell only knew she might shoot me for him running away. Such a soiled pretty thing I could not believe how she'd ever survive living on her father's ranch now that she was back in Texas. Well, she was no ward of mine—thank God.

I gathered my hat, brushed the dry grass and dirt off it, then put it on my head. When I reached Beggar, I stepped in the saddle and watched her re-holster her six-gun.

"If you'd drop all the charges against me, I'd take you home."

Hands on her slim hips I got that same damn scowl again. "I don't want one damn thing from you mister."

"I can promise you those new boots will blister your feet walking that far in them."

"How far do you think it is?"

"Well, Loretta, it is about ten miles back to your headquarters." I booted him to go and headed south—her direction.

"Wait for me."

I stopped him. "You want to ride with me?"

"Yes."

I waited. Never turned back like I planned to go on.

"All right, mister. I won't charge you with that."

"Won't charge me with raping you. Call me Clint."

"All right, Clint. I won't charge you."

"Will you dance with me next Saturday night at the Daisy Creek School house?"

"I didn't plan to attend it."

I booted Beggar with my spur.

"All right. I will dance with you wherever."

I swung him around. "The Daisy Creek School house potluck and dance Saturday night."

"Yes, there."

I reined Beggar around to face her and repeated the event again.

"All right—Daisy Creek potluck and dance—I will dance with you there next Saturday night."

"Good. Can I eat supper with you too?"

"Yes, you may."

I moved him closer dropped my arm down for her and swung her up behind me.

"Keep your heels out of his flank. He's real goosey—"

Beggar gave one hop, and I checked him.

"I know. Don't put my heels in his flank."

"Right. Now, Beggar, let's go to her house."

We rode a mile or so, and she tried not to make contact with me riding atop my bedroll back there. Hard to do that. And her form occasionally made an impression on my back—nice deal. When I started up a short cut, she had to hug me with him going uphill.

"You took this way on purpose—"

"Shush. I heard something." I stopped him to listen. "Get off."

"I can hear cattle bawling. Why?" she whispered to me beside the horse.

"They are being herded. We may get to see who is doing this."

"You think it's rustlers?"

I held my finger to her mouth. She quieted, and I hitched him. Then we got down and crawled through under the cedars and live oak. On the crest, I motioned for her to get down. Obviously, someone or more were driving cattle north up this valley, and I wanted a sight of them.

"What can we do?" she hissed.

I cupped my hand to her ear. "All we need is a good look at them. You and I can't whip hard case rustlers up here."

One was coming closer, and I shoved her down. We lay on the pungent cedar needles. My six-gun in my sweaty hand. We were too close to him when he rode by on a bay horse. I saw the curled-up brim on the back of his hat and the red bandana. I could find him lined up at any saloon bar.

"Why didn't you shoot him?"

"Because—" I quieted her with a finger. Two more riders passed by. One horse had a white sock on his right foot.

"Too many."

She swallowed and quick like agreed with a nod. We waited until they were gone up the canyon.

"Where will they take them?"

"I don't know, but we might track them tomorrow."

"Why not now?"

The rustlers were beyond hearing when I set her up. "Number one, you are a girl. Those bas—outlaws would hurt you if I failed. Too big a risk for one man against the three or more of them."

Her blue eyes could get set so quick and mad at me. "And me along stopped you?"

"That's my story, and I am certain someone can catch them."

"Who will catch them?"

"Your father and his men. We have a description."

She shook her head in disgust and struggled to her feet once out from under the tree. "I am not some China doll."

Brushing the needles off my shirtfront I motioned to the horse. "No, but I'm not telling your dad I got you shot either."

In the saddle, I hauled her up, ducked some branches, and we rode off the hillside.

It was past sundown when the dogs welcomed us at their headquarters. Bare headed, her six-foot tall dad came out on the porch lighted by the open door. "Where you two been? Out snipe hunting?"

"My horse didn't come home?" she asked looking around in the dark

"No. That you, Clint?"

"Yes, sir."

"Thanks for bringing her home."

"Tell him what we found?" she said to me.

"Three rustlers were herding cattle north today."

He gave a rueful head sake. "Come inside. I'll see if we can follow them in the morning. You two haven't had supper, have you?"

She looked at me and said, "No."

"Carla, these two need some food. Come on in, Clint. What about the rustlers?"

"I was coming back, and we met at the pipe spring. Her horse ran off, and I was bringing her home when we heard them over the hill moving cattle north. I didn't want to butt in with her along, but I saw one guy had a turned up back brim hat I'd recognize and another rode a bay horse with a white right hind sock."

"Thanks. I'm glad to have my daughter back safe."

"I asked her to attend the Daisy Creek Schoolhouse dance next Saturday night if that is all right?"

"Certainly." He hugged her shoulder. "Carla has some food ready."

I didn't miss seeing her looking at the ceiling for help over his casually agreeing to her going with me.

"Will that horse come home?" she asked him.

"He'll be here by daylight."

"Good."

The three of us sat down. He drank coffee, and we ate some good food.

"I can't believe you two met out there, and then you found the rustlers too."

I couldn't either.

SATURDAY MORNING, I BORROWED MY neighbor's buckboard and team to go pickup Miss Priss at her place, the Y Bar Y Ranch, and then drive her to the dance. This was going to be a I-showed-you-so sort of deal. I had no idea how bad this might turn out. Be a lot less than anything she knew from going to finishing school.

She was ready when I arrived, and a kitchen worker put two baskets of food in the back.

"That's our lunch, and the food for the potluck."

"Sounds great. That is sure a nice blue dress."

"You don't have to compliment me. As I recall, you blackmailed me into doing this."

"I suppose you had an offer to go to the opera tonight?"

"Anyone ever tell you that you are impossible?"

"No."

"Have you ever had a wife or girlfriend before?"

"I was engaged once. The Comanche killed her."

Her look at me turned to sad. "I am sorry."

"So was I." I clucked to the team to make them trot.

"Clint, can you talk about it?"

"Myra Calico was eighteen. I met her at roundup. She was helping cook for all the cowboys. We struck up a friendship and went to dances when I could get over there. Her family lived about thirty miles west of here. We made plans to be married the next spring. That was in October two years ago. The Comanche made a fall raid under a full moon in November. They massacred her entire family. We never found her body. Is that good enough?"

"She must have been a strong person. Your story about her has about made me cry."

"No need in that. She is with the good Lord, and I have been sentenced to live without her."

She reached over and hugged my arm. Never said another word for several miles. There was a place on the road to San Antonio where there was a hand pump and shade. I told her we'd stop there and have some lunch.

"Nice of you to think of that."

When I stopped, she stood up to get down. "You better thank Carla, Dad's housekeeper, for that. I'm afraid you'd have had jelly sandwiches if I did it."

I don't know if I was supposed to laugh or not, but I took her by the waist and set her down from off the buckboard. That took her back too, I could tell, that I could lift her and easy set her down on her feet. But I let it go. She didn't need much to get her mad.

To prepare a place to picnic, she spread a blanket on the short-cropped grass and put down a wicker basket. Napkin, China plates, silverware, silver tumblers for glasses—I sat down cross legged.

"Would you ask grace?"

I swallowed and quickly agreed.

"Want to get on our knees and hold hands?"

"Why sure." I moved closer, and we held hands. "Lord, Loretta and I are here today on a trip to meet our neighbors and celebrate life here on earth. I want you to help Paul Green who was in a horse wreck and needs your help. Granny Martin has a bad heart that needs to be stronger. Lord, be in the heart of this young lady and mine as we go through our lives here today. For us to be generous with the downtrodden and those who really need help. In his name we pray—amen."

"Clint, you did well. I guess he will bless our food."

I'd sat back down on my heels and shook my head. "I haven't done a lot of praying out loud. I had a lot to try to cover, and plumb forgot the food."

She kissed me on the forehead. "I liked what you said about us in your prayer. I can't say you were in my heart until you said that—thank you. You are a very complex man. I understand about your loss, and I am not used to cowboys, but this afternoon—I see you in a different light."

"I didn't say that to change you in any way. But if we are going to share some time, I want you to respect me as well as I will respect you."

"Thank you." She turned away, and I knew she was crying.

On my knees, I waded over and hugged her shoulders. "Loretta, we come to have some fun and live a little today. It ain't a sad deal. I didn't ask you to come up here to cry. I like you laughing and smiling better."

Wet eyes, I dabbed her cheeks easy with my handkerchief.

She nodded and took it from me. "I'll try to do better."

"Maybe you should tell me about your mother."

"Oh, Clint, my mother divorced my father when I was eleven. He took my custody. She went to Tucson to meet, I understand, her lover. Dad decided I needed to go to a finishing school to save me turning out like my mother—later. I wrote her letters when I could find her address, but she never answered them. Their divorce was not my fault. What she did was wrong, but I did not have to wear her shoes either."

"That is not your fault at all. We can only live our own lives."

She put her hand on my shoulder. "We're learning lot's. I have some sausage sandwiches on Carla's sourdough bread."`

"Sounds good to me."

WE ARRIVED AT THE SCHOOLHOUSE in late afternoon, and she took her pies in the other basket Carla had fixed. I knew all those wives would have to quiz her. I only hoped she could take it and did not get mad. Her trigger temper could explode awful easy.

I talked to some of my single pals who asked where I got her.

Clyde Dawes said, "Why that's Miss Loretta fresh from finishing school in St Louis. Boys, he's done horned the rest of you out from her."

"I wish him luck. She's way too high priced for me." Jed Clayton shook his head. "Clint how did you ever meet her?"

"I stopped by and took a drink at a spring. Her horse ran off, and I offered her a ride home. We about stumbled on some rustlers stealing their cattle."

"You try to stop them?" Clyde asked me.

I shook my head. "Too many with her there. Howard and his men will get them later. But he said they lost their tracks north of there."

"If the sheriff had any real help, they could stop them," Jed said.

I set in on them, "Guys, we all know the sheriff has too much country. And we won't have any law in Texas till them carpetbaggers leave Austin and we get the Rangers back. Or we form our own county out here."

"Yeah, Jed, but we may be old men by then," Clyde said.

"What we need is a real posse, and root every petty thief, troublemaker, and possible rustler out of this county."

"Vigilante law would have troops of black soldiers camped here forever."

I'd heard enough, so in a guarded voice I said, "I say we shut up talking here and meet somewhere next Thursday night we know is secure and form a group to end this problem. Start with the bunch stealing Howard Stone's stock. But don't everyone ride to that place together, bring a flour sack mask and a rifle, plus a bed roll in case we need it. We clean that bunch up. We can herd the others out after that."

"Only bring tight mouthed men. Any doubt, don't bring them," Clyde said.

I agreed.

"Will Howard come?"

"I'll talk to him. He wants rid of them badly. You'll know others. Just be damn selective like Clyde said."

After looking around the three of us split up. I went to find Loretta. My belly was growling, and she met me coming inside and smiling.

"Everyone acted pleased I came. Clint, I am grateful you brought me."

"Good. I figured you'd like it here. This is Texas social society. These people all work hard, and this is the outlet for that."

"There is a preacher going to say grace next. I was going to get you."

"Hope he remembers the food."

She shook her head and smiled.

"Our Father who art in heaven—" he began, and everyone inside joined him in the Lord's Prayer. "Let's eat this wonderful food."

I noticed this time she had tin plates for this meal. Not being too fancy over here. I showed her my tin plate and said, "Thanks."

Her hip to mine waiting in line, she nodded like she understood. They taught her a lot in that school. She never had a mom growing up—that was hard to believe. My mom had lots to do with even my life as a boy at that age. I know she coached my sisters—all of them settled down, married, and had strong families that I knew about. Sounded to me like Loretta missed all that growing up. But she sure was an eye-catcher in that bright blue dress.

We filled our plates. There were worlds of food on those long tables, and we found a spot on the benches on the wall. She set her plate down and took two silver cups for our lemonade. Before she left, she leaned in close. "There weren't any tin cans I could find."

"Oh, to drink out of. That's fine."

"You sure?"

"Absolutely."

"Good." She went on with them.

We talked to the couples on both sides while we ate. How did you two meet? Had we known each other long? Did we have any plans?

"We're here to greet and meet folks and find out if we can even dance."

This one straight backed lady on my left—Mrs. Jennings said, "I've danced with him before, and you can dance with him."

"Good news. I've worried all the way over here about that." Then she waved her hands. It was only a joke, and they laughed.

"You sure needed to." I went on eating and received an elbow for it and a grin.

Not a whole lot of humor comes into my life. This we found, and it warmed me—being there with her and it working so far. I worried about my small herd of cattle on the range and breaking horses. I did that for scratch money. Something always comes along requires money, so breaking and trading horses finances those things. I also have some Mexican cattle fattening on the range beside my cows and calves. I am what the big ranchers call a two-bit outfit, but I do my share at roundup and make my part work.

My brand, the Quarter Circle X, is respected and a hard one to work over though there were brand forgers could change about any brand to something else. And despite everyone's efforts there was rustling going on. There's some rustling going on about all the time.

They call it *don't eat your own beef.*

I was pretty enthralled with finding her after our rough start. And after she washed our silverware and plates, she set them in a cloth sack under the bench. We waltzed to the fiddle music, and I felt I'd gone to heaven and died. She was like a feather to dance with, and her blue eyes sparkled the further we went around the floor. By the time I was eight years old, my three older sisters had me practicing with them humming a tune. We took up the rag rug and danced. The three wore me out back then, but while that was work, if they hadn't, I'd never waltzed that evening with her.

Then my single pals found us. They took turns dancing and laughing with her, and I got to dance with Mrs. Jennings,

We were circling the floor full of dancers and Mrs. Jennings very perfectly said, "I think they have you treed, Clint."

They'd done it. That's when a hunting hound has a coon up a tree and stays there barking until you come shoot it out. I was treed. But when I came back, I instructed those two that I got every other dance with her and for them to dance with Mrs. Jennings whose husband had two left feet.

Loretta was amused when we got ready, and they shouted, "Polka time."

Boy, I swung her laughing around that schoolhouse dance floor. There wasn't a German couple there could out dance us. And we were both out of breath when we staggered back, and she held up her hands in surrender. "I need to sit this one out,"

So, we sat the next one out and sat holding each other's hands like we were afraid the other one would run off.

"Your friends are very nice men. They really appreciate you. Are there not any girls their own age around here?" she asked me.

"You look around. Most girls get married very young out here. There are not many left for them unless they want to raise a wife."

"Then I am an old maid?"

"Going on that," I said.

Got an elbow for that too.

She smiled at my pals and took me by the hand back to dance with her.

"Why didn't we bring bedrolls to sleep in?"

I frowned at her. "I didn't want to ruin your reputation."

"Nice work, but we will be all night getting back home."

"Next time I will ask you. This time I was pleased I'd blackmailed you into dancing with me."

"You are right, if I had not met you at the spring, I'd have probably told you no. If you hadn't located those rustlers so slick and took me home so nicely—I wouldn't have come here with you and had the time of my life. Besides, I was out riding out of boredom, and you damn sure woke me up. Also, since I came home, I curse like my father does. For you I will try to do better."

And around the floor we went like no one was there but the two of us. I'd never had that feeling before with anyone. Not even when I courted the one I lost.

With her settled in, my mind turned to how to handle the vigilante issue next. Her dad had been around. I bet he could help me with the law enforcement part. I'd ask him to.

"You worried about going home tonight?"

"Not with you, but we can be more practical next time. I do thank you—"

My finger stopped her. "Loretta. I respect you. I won't put your honor to any test that might smear your reputation."

"How many sisters did you have?"

"Three older and two younger."

"What did they do?"

"From eight on I had to dance with 'em at home even."

On her feet laughing, she asked, "Will I get to meet them?"

"I suppose—" Then I stopped her. "There's a fight outside. I better go break it up."

"Don't get hurt. You have to drive me home still tonight."

I waved that I heard her. And I slipped through the onlookers in the doorway and took the steps two at a time, and in the bonfire's life I saw about four men throwing fists.

"Clyde, give me a hand. Break this up. We came here for fun not fighting."

I jerked one fighter down on his butt and met his opponent face to face. "Quit. I mean it—now."

"You ain't the gawdamn law up here. Ain't none of your damned business."

"Quit cussing too. There are children here." He drew back to hit me. I hit him with a haymaker blow to his upper belly and the air went out of him, bent him over and my knee smashed his face putting him on his back holding up his hands and begging me to stop.

I swept up his hat and shoved it at him. "Load up and get out of here. Don't come back till you can act decent."

By then, I had enough enforcers to back me. They retreated and left grumbling. I held up my hands. "We don't need fighting or cussing with all these ladies and children here. You see anyone doing that report it to one of us before it starts."

Someone clapped and then everyone clapped—but the sight that got to me the most was Loretta standing there with my pistol. I'd put it under the buckboard seat when we first got there—no need to pack it there.

"Thanks, I won't need it now." Then I saw her face, and I hugged and kissed her. "The deal's over. But it was sure sweet of you to fetch it for me."

Her eyes closed, and she nodded. "I know who you are now."

"I'm what?"

"There was a certain kind of hero I once read about in English history. You're my knight in armor."

I began shaking my head at her. "Aw, Loretta, I just want things to go right."

"You can't compliment him for a thing, Loretta. You just have to accept him like he is. Trust me. We've tried," my pal Jed said.

"Thank you, Jed. I appreciate you guys for helping him too. Those guys were tough that you ran off."

"Why, Loretta, they weren't half as bad as the Taggot brothers. Were they, Clint? Why we got our clothing about tore off our backs fighting them one night. Them big old boys really liked to fight. Folks say when they can't' fight anyone else, they fight themselves."

His story had her laughing. She stood on her toes and kissed that tall galoot on the cheek. Hell, after doing that, he'd have broke his neck for anything she wanted.

"We better go inside. I'll hang this gun up on the hat rack just in case."

I herded both of them inside. The trouble was over, I hoped. It had been a great evening for me aside from those four troublemakers.

The longest trip you ever take is always going home. She got so sleepy for a while she slept with her head in my lap, and I worried we'd hit a bump and throw her on the floor. No telling. The moon had gone down, and the stars weren't real bright. Many hours later, I got down, and after hushing the dogs, I carried her in my arms into the house.

"Where is your bed?" I asked.

"Top of stairs—put me down. You may fall."

I set her down. She grasped my hand and pulled me after her. Up we went and the starlight showed on the bed.

"Shed your boots. We can sleep in our clothes."

"We can't do that here."

"Shed your damn boots. I need you to hold me. I am shaking inside."

She wasn't the only one shaking. I toed off my boots and followed her to the bed. We kissed and then I took her in my arms and wrapped her up tight.

After a time, the shaking eased, then stopped entirely. Soon after came the soft sound of snoring.

It was the sweetest sound I'd ever heard.

Oh my God, what a deal to hold....

IT WAS DAYLIGHT AND SOMEONE was talking to us. She and I fully dressed in each other's arms—on the bed.

"You two missed a good sermon at church this morning. Carla has lunch ready. You two alive?" That was Howard in a suit standing in the bedroom doorway. My vision was not clear, but he did not hold a shotgun in his arms like I would have at this point if she'd been my daughter.

She sat up and tried to clear her eyes. "It is all his fault—" Then she broke out laughing.

"No harm done. Bring him along. She has a nice meal for all of us."

I could hear him chuckling going down the stairs.

She shoved me back down and kissed me hard. "I never had a better time in my entire life. Let me brush my hair. You were great. I would never have slept if you had not held me."

The dress straightened, her hair brushed hard and fast, she smiled and led the way. Stopping to be sure I was coming. "You sleep all right?"

"No."

"What was wrong?"

"Someday I will tell you—go on. It is too long to even start here."

At the bottom, she hugged my arm and whispered, "I can make it up to you."

Smiling at her back we went apart into the dining room.

"Obviously you two had a good evening. Clint, we pray before we eat."

"That's fine."

He gave a short one.

We began to pass things.

For her and me from there on, after Sunday dinner, things went fast and furious. Before a week went by our marriage plans were set, but I never regretted any of it. I have a loving, smart wife and the vigilante moves we made following our wedding ran off the rustlers. Things are a lot more settled, and the formation of a county is at hand. Folks say I'll be the first sheriff. Good thing I have her.

HE NEVER FORGOT THAT RAID

IRA FALLON WANTED FOR YEARS growing up to forget the night when those thugs hired by the big rancher, Samuel Gordon, came to their unfinished sod house to run off his family with their ear shattering screams that woke him up that night. They beat his father senseless, raped his fifteen-year-old sister, Jenny, slapped his mother around, then told her if they didn't move off their homestead in twenty-four hours, they'd come back and kill every one of them. They kicked and beat the hell out of him for tackling them like he was going to stop them.

He had a bad scar on the left side of his mouth that any look in a mirror reminded him who they were who did that.

On a small pad, he kept their names. Gordon Sanchez had been the leader, Romero O'Brian his henchman. Red Lockhart, Fred Angles, Bud Hall, Chico Farnum, Tad Green, and the Pecos Kid.

In those next few years, his father died, and his mother remarried. His older sister went to work in a cathouse, and Ira Fallon learned how to shoot a gun, how to fight with a knife or a club. He could out draw the fastest men he ever met and could put five bullets in a dancing tin can.

Ira was second in command of the Texas Rafter K's two thousand head of longhorn steers delivered to Abilene, Kansas, in 1867. Foreman Big Jim

Dodson paid him forty bucks a month for his effort. That job complete he found a low place with a grassy hill for his shooting range and two sacks of brown bottles. His helper, Ned Roland, set up the bottles for him to shoot at.

The tow-headed kid about sixteen years old told him he was an orphan and took up with him shortly after they met in Abilene. Seated on the log, Ira busily reloaded his .44 cap and ball Colts. He wanted more accuracy in his shooting.

With the bottles set up on the board they found to use for a rack, Ned came back and sat on his butt hugging his knees. "You figure you're getting better at this shooting?"

"That's why we're here. To tune it up more before we pull out for Texas."

He snapped the pistol's loading lever closed and holstered it. On his feet, he felt ready. In a flash, he whipped out his six gun and fanning the hammer each time he shot, he mowed down four of five bottles in an instant.

"Darn, that was good."

"No. He shook his head. "I need to hit all five."

"Where are these guys at?"

"Texas, Mexico, El Paso. We'll find them."

"Are they all still alive?"

"I am not sure. But we will find them if you want to go along with me."

"I would like to."

Ira made a hard nod. "It will be bloody, or I'll be dead."

"I'd hate that."

"Just the way things go." Ira shrugged.

So, they rode south from Abilene, retracing his ride across the plains with two packhorses and making good time.

"Was there something in those letters from that old ranger to help you find them?" Ned asked.

"He found a few of them. One's in San Antonio. Fred Angles. He gave me an address where he's living."

"What will he do when you confront him?"

"Either he'll deny it or piss in his pants."

Ned laughed.

"I'm not kidding. These bastards ruined my life and my family's lives as well."

Ned nodded. "Do they know about you?"

"I don't think so. They ran several families off that land until Samuel Gordon was able to buy all that acreage for cents on the dollar from the state of Texas."

"You ever meet any of them?"

"No. I've been busy preparing myself to face them down."

"You consider yourself a one-man army?"

"If I have to be. What these bastards did was a crime, and no law would stop them."

"But Gordon's real rich, and he can hire more guns."

"Let him hire them. A smart man told me everyone has an unguarded spot."

"You know where they are?"

"I will find them."

Ned shrugged. "I appreciate you for caring for me. I don't know if I'm tough enough to assist you, but I can hold the horses."

"I won't ask nothing from you. But thanks."

They reached San Antonio and boarded their horses with a man who Ira knew at the outskirts. Then they set out to find Angles. He lived in a *barrio* neighborhood. They ate with a woman street merchant with a small firebox sitting on the curb close to his address. She cooked the spiced beef strips and made great flour tortillas to wrap them with some fried onions and peppers.

Ira, in Spanish, asked if she knew this guy, Angles.

"He is a mean dog. He kicks women who get in his way and small children. Why do you ask?"

"He gave me this scar." He pointed to his cheek.

She understood his cause. "No one would miss him if his throat was cut."

He nodded. "Say nothing."

"My lips are sealed."

"Bueno. Gracias."

They found that Angles went to a *cantina* every day until he was drunk and then staggered home like a mad dog knocking down innocent people and kicking them.

People avoided him if they knew it was him coming. After three nights watching him and listening to him thrashing his woman each time he got home, he told Ned it was time to end his mean-miserable life on this earth.

They were ready on the fourth night and ushered him into the alley with a gun barrel poked in his side.

"Do you know who I am?"

"No," he slurred.

"I am the boy you kicked many times up on Duck Creek at our homestead. You remember that night?"

"No."

Ira kneed him in the crotch. That bent Angles over holding his balls.

"You kicked me there over and over. Remember?"

"No."

"Well, you will die thinking about me and my family that you ruined." He holstered his gun and swept the blade of his super sharp Bowie knife across Angles belly and spilled his guts out.

Ira turned to his helper. "Time to go. He won't forget me again."

The night soon swallowed them. They slept in a loft and walked to where their horses were stabled the next day. When they were saddled and the packhorses loaded, Ned asked him where they would go next?

"A village south of here. San Alberto."

"Who is there?"

"Chico Farnum has a place there."

"You recall what he looks like?"

"Their faces are engraved in my brain."

Late afternoon, they rode up the fenced lane to a paint-less grey farmhouse. A Mexican woman came to the open door.

"Is Chico here?" He leaned over the great wooden saddle horn.

Her reply that he was not there came in Spanish.

She was either pregnant or potbellied.

"You need my body?" she finally asked.

"Ned, ask her what she charges?"

His Spanish was very well done. "What do you charge?"

Her reply was fifty cents.

He dug out two quarters and gave them to the boy with a head toss for him to use her. "Take your time. I bet he does not return until dark."

He dismounted. Hitched their horses while Ned and his hostess went inside jabbering in Spanish. Seated under a cottonwood tree, their horses stood hipshot at the rack. He whittled and listened to the leaves along with the shouting and laughter coming from the house.

Ned didn't return. He had whittled on many sticks when a rider came up the drive. He looked half asleep in the saddle. When he got close, he stopped the horse and looked suspiciously at Ira as he rose to his feet.

"You doing business here?"

"My *compadre* is."

Chico kind of digested that and dismounted. "You already use her?"

Ira shook his head.

Chico was dressed in dirty white clothing and strapped on sandals. He lifted his shirt and tightened his rope belt up some on his belly. "Your boss in there?

"He is not my boss."

"How did you find her?"

"She answered the door."

Chico sat on a crate. "I found her in Chihuahua."

"Do you remember me?"

"No. Should I?"

"Remember when you worked for Samuel Gordon of the SGR ranch?"

"I think so."

"Oh, you recall running them homesteaders off his place."

"Yeah. We did many."

"You remember kicking a ten-year-old boy?"

"No. But we only got paid if those squatters moved out."

"They moved?"

"Oh, yeah, or we went back and shot them."

"You kicked me that night."

"Must have been another guy done that."

"No, you had boots on that night."

"I had forgotten—it has been a long time ago."

"I didn't forget that night."

"What do you want from me?"

Ira folded his knife and dropped it in his vest pocket. Then he drew his six gun that smelled of oil and gun smoke.

Chico held out his hands to stop him as he eased the hammer back. "Mother of God, don't kill me. I have some money. I can pay you."

"How much?"

"Two hundred, maybe more."

"Any tricks, and you are dead. Show me the money."

"Don't shoot me."

"Get going." He waved the barrel at him to move.

At the barn, in some straw, the outlaw found a mason jar and with shaking hands handed it to Ira.

"That is all my savings."

It was heavy with gold coins and some paper money. Ira noticed some blacksmith tools in the building. He made Chico stand at the center post in the room that held the barn roof up.

"What are you going to do to me?" he asked while he tied the man's hands behind his back.

Ira noticed the raider was already pissing on himself. He holstered his gun and when he was satisfied with him being tied, he went for some horse hoof nippers. He told Chico to open his mouth. The man's eyes flew open.

"You won't forget me when you don't have front teeth to eat with."

Crunching off his front teeth in the great pinchers even with him tied was a hard fought, screaming struggle, but at last he had cut off his upper four center teeth and blood covered the outlaw's mouth. Chico sounded hoarse from screaming.

"I bet you remember kicking me now."

Ned sat his horse at the barn door with the packhorses and Ira's mount.

Ira came out and took the reins.

"He needed some dentistry work?" Ned asked.

Ira dumped the contents of the jar into his saddlebags. "I took up a collection for doing it, too."

They rode on.

In a week, they learned that Red and Bud frequented a whorehouse across the Rio Grande near Slatter's Store. Saturday night was those two's night to visit the lively *cantina*. From the shade of a closed store across the street they waited for the two to arrive.

Red rode a paint horse, so in the moonlight, they could easily recognize him. It was past dark when the two arrived at the Roho Cantina. The two hitched their jaded ponies at the crowded rack, and laughing, went inside.

He and Ned crossed the street, and he told Ned to watch for and to learn where Hall went with his *puta*. He'd do the same with Red. In a short while, Red talked to the bartender who obviously told him his favorite bed partner was in the back.

Ira followed him and knew what crib he went into. He went back out into the smoky *cantina* where he saw Hall and a sassy dove head for the hallway. Ned followed them.

When Ned came back. Without words, together they went to Red's girl's room. At the door, they heard Red was busy on top of his partner. They silenced both of them with their cocked gun barrels ready to blow them to hell.

Ned stripped a sheet and soon bound and gagged her face down on the bed.

Then he held his gun while Ira gagged the naked Red with his hands tied behind his back. Ira went and did the same to Hall who also was busy inside of his woman. He knocked Hall in the head unconscious, then gagged and tied her in sheet strips. With the groggy prisoner naked and gagged, hands tied behind him, when the coast was clear Ira took him along. A knock brought Ned with his prisoner out in the hall, and they took the two naked men out the rear door.

A block away Ned went for their horses. When he came back, they put lariats around both men's necks and tied them so they couldn't be opened.

"We are leading you off our horses. If you fall or can't keep up we will drag you until you die. Savvy?"

They both nodded and gagged with their hands tied behind their backs they could follow or die. Ira showed them no mercy and had them running part of the time. They reached a deserted place out of town, and the outlaws crumbled to the ground.

Ned lit a coal oil lamp that he tied on a limb for light. Then, one at a time, they drug their naked prisoners to stakes driven in the ground and tied them spread eagled stretched out on their backs. When they were both tied securely, Ned ungagged them.

"You guys remember me?" Ira asked. "You two were working for Samuel running off settlers filing homesteads on his range. You recall that night you two raped a fifteen-year-old innocent girl?"

"No," Red said.

"She was my sister. And you shamed her so bad that night she's become a prostitute. A perfectly innocent girl who you two treated like a Mexican *puta*."

"You've got the wrong guys," Red said.

"No, I don't. When I am done gelding both of you, every time you reach to scratch your privates you will recall that night 'cause you won't have any."

"I got money. I can pay you."

"Where?'

"Sewed in my saddle blanket. Take me back to my horse."

Ira looked in the orange glow of the lamp over at Ned. "We can check that out."

Ned smugly agreed.

"You bastards," Red swore.

"No, you are them." Ira bent over grasped Hall's scrotum and sliced the bottom off of it. Then with Hall screeching for help, he deftly removed each seed like he'd done colts and tossed them aside.

"I'll get your ass for this," Red said through his teeth.

"You won't forget raping her though." Then one by one he pulled Red's out holding the seeds tight in his fist.

Loud as Red screamed they might have heard him a thousand miles west at Juarez. Job complete, Ira washed his bloody hands under water from a canteen Ned held.

"Two more will remember that night as long as they live."

Hands dried they left them tied in their agony and rode back to town. Ira removed the saddle from the paint and saddle bags off his saddle and rolled it up. Then they did the same to Hall's outfit. When they were done, Ira took the headstalls off both of their horses and freed them into the night.

One border town newspaper called it the bloodiest crime in Texas history. Masked raiders kidnapped these two respected businessmen, took them to an undisclosed site and castrated them, taking all their money and jewelry."

"Jewelry?" Ned asked after Ira read it to him from the San Antonio edition.

"Diamond rings and watches I guess."

Ned laughed. "They called them businessmen?"

"I guess we must be too. We've got enough money to buy us a good ranch up around Fort Worth. And we can get the other after things cool down."

Ned agreed.

They stopped in Marble Falls. Ira had a tip that his sister, Jenny, might be working there. The two-story house had a red lamp on the porch when they hitched their horses out front. Wasn't any trade parked there. With hats in hand, they climbed the steps, and the black house-girl showed them inside.

"Is Jenny here?"

"Yas sah, she be napping."

"Take me up there. I want to surprise her." He handed her a silver dollar too.

Ned stayed to talk to the three doves in the parlor.

The girl knocked. "Miss Jenny. Your friend Ira be here to see you."

It took her a minute or so to get to the door.

"I don't know any—Ira! What are you doing here?"

He hugged her tight to his chest. "Ned and I are going north to buy a ranch. We want you to cook for us."

"I am not a cook."

"Well, you soon will be one. Gather your things. You won't have to entertain any more drunks."

"Why me?"

"'Cause we're blood kin. I know a lot of water's gone under the bridge. We are all three going to start over on a new place."

"Do you have a wife?"

"Not yet."

"Can I pick one out for you tonight who really wants a man?"

"I guess. You'll like Ned."

She had Ira by the hand. "I bet I can please him. You'll like Rose Mary."

At the second door, she knocked and then twisted the knob, and the prettiest six-foot-tall naked young woman stood up, looking steaming mad at their intrusion.

"What is this?" she demanded.

Oh my God! He looked for her wings. She must have been an angel.

"My brother is here. He wants you to join us. You said you really wanted a husband. He and his buddy are buying a ranch. He'll marry you."

She cried, then ran over and hugged him. Their mouths met, and he held all that wonderful flesh in his hands.

"Quit. We've got time for that later. Dress and pack up. We're going to Fort Worth."

Ned was in the doorway looking pleased.

"That's Jenny. Help her pack. I'll bring this one."

Ned took her hand, then they melted together, and he kissed her. To Ira they looked like they both were love struck.

"Get moving."

"We are. We are." They ran off.

Rose was about dressed. "Is this dress I have on good enough to wear in public?"

"It is plenty good enough."

"Turn your back. I have to pee." She drug the pot out from under the bed and squatted over it.

Why he had to do that when he had seen all of her before, he had no idea?

They quickly had her two bags packed. She said she'd never wear some of the stuff, but she was taking it along anyway.

Then in the doorway, like a stern sheriff with her back straight and her almost exposed bust was no doubt the madam. "What in Hell is going on up here?"

"Meet my husband to be, Ira."

"He ain't taking you nowhere. You signed a contract to stay here for another year."

Ira set down her two large suitcases. "I didn't catch your name?"

"Quendaline."

"Quen, all I need to do is bust a few coal oil lamps, and you won't have a whorehouse. It will burn down fast. Now, don't challenge her, me or Jenny and Ned."

"They've both signed contracts."

"I am tearing them up. Now get the hell out of the road."

She did step aside for the two of them. Rose didn't have her shoes completely buttoned, but she came wobbling after him with a large bag and purse.

The madam was screaming bloody murder about someone stopping them. But no one did, and the other girls in the parlor hugged them and their past workers as well.

Madam's final charge came at them from the porch. "You two whores won't ever get a job in another respectable whore house in Texas. I will see to that."

Rose nodded. "I guess I'll have to be a wife for the rest of my life since I won't be able to work in a respectable one ever again."

The suitcases hooked on their saddles and leading the horses, they went to the livery, bought a surrey and a nice team of horses.

Once outside of town, they slept with their men in their bedrolls. Ned cooked breakfast, and they loaded up for Fort Worth. The honeymoon lasted five days, and they found a grassy place with a large farmhouse for a thousand dollars in Coleman County. The rest of Red's money also bought two sections of partially fenced grassland with some water.

The men bought every cheap heifer they could find priced from two to ten dollars a head to stock it. They used an old wagon to haul them home. The women grew great gardens on the home place. Twice a week they sold their produce in town.

They weren't getting rich but both women said they'd never go back to their old trade, and both couples finally were married in a double wedding in a church. No one would recognize their two wives from their past. They dressed like farm wives and both soon were pregnant.

Everything went fine after that.

———————————

WORD SOON BEGAN TO CIRCULATE that the Pecos Kid was robbing banks all over and was wanted real bad by the law everywhere. Tad Green was listed, as his partner along with some other outlaws wanted in the Indian Territory as well.

Ira started back up his letter writing to find where they might be. One man he trusted and had paid for information said they worked out of somewhere near Fort Supply on Wolf Creek in the Indian Territory.

Ira laid out plans. He hired three good men to watch his growing herd of cows and the two women and babies. Jenny and Rose were upset but understood how they felt about those two. Wells Fargo had five-thousand-dollar rewards on both of their heads.

"We have to act fast. Every old badge toter between here and California will be coming after those two at those prices."

They rushed up there in ten days and had them pinpointed at a small horse ranch west of Fort Supply. After scoping it for a few days, they decided all the wanted outlaws were in their nest.

He and Ned took out the two nightguards, then they moved on to the house. The three sleeping in hammocks in the yard were knocked unconscious and handcuffed plus leg irons and gagged.

That left the Kid and Tad sleeping with women in the house. Ned took Tad. Ira went in for the Kid. They entered both bedrooms. Ira took no chances and knocked the Kid out cold and handcuffed his wife to the bed and gagged her, then he manacled the groggy Kid both hands and legs.

He was curious about his partner. He found Tad in irons, belly down on the floor beside his wife. She'd been gagged.

"Come on. We need to find his loot."

They took the Kid down to the horse tank and after a short while near drowning him in a horse tank he sputtered out where to find it.

Once they'd dug it up, they couldn't believe the amount of loot the Kid had acquired during his career. Much of it was gold.

Ned made a trip to town and bought two used crates and rented a large team of mules and a stout wagon to drive back to where it had been hidden. They loaded the gold and currency in the crates and nailed them shut. But not before they put some fresh sheep hides in each box and marked them *SHEEP FAT* on the sides. They shipped them from a railroad station across the line in Kansas. It cost two hundred bucks to ship them to Ira at West Creek Station, Texas.

The eight prisoners and their wives were all in handcuffs and leg irons. They were hauled in both wagons to Fort Supply, and the U.S. Marshals in Dewey were sent to take all the prisoners into custody. By that point, Ira and Ned needed a break. Their captives had begun to stink to high heaven.

He and Ned filled out the papers. The Army stationed there incarcerated them for the authorities. The federal and Wells Fargo reward papers turned in, they climbed on their horses and packhorses and rode home.

Two weeks later, they rode into the ranch yard and the sheep fat boxes had beat them. Both women kissed their husbands and pinched their noses at the smelly freight. Meanwhile, Ira handed out twenties to all the men for the great job they did guarding things while they were gone that month. They saddled up and went to get treated and drunk in town.

Ned and Jenny were off getting caught up in bed. He knew that Rose wanted to do the same thing, and she wondered why he was going to open those stinky crates.

He made her get on a ladder to see it. He pried the lid up, and her eyes bugged out.

"Oh, my God, darling. How much is there?"

"I have no idea. But not counting the rewards, we are rich."

They danced in the dust, and Ira nailed the top back down. Rose made him go upstairs with her and break in on the lovers so she could tell Jenny how much sheep fat they had.

SHEEP FAT BECAME THEIR NAME for it. Ira worked closely with his banker to get the money back into circulation and had money in several banks. But traces of the sheep perfume were obvious to customers in the local bank on hot days.

The banker said, "That just proves sheep are a good healthy business."

But good fortune came their way. Ira learned Samuel Gordon must have fallen on some hard times and poor investments. They learned that, if he didn't pay off his investors, he faced prison time for fraud. Texas courts were tough on swindlers and robbers, putting them away like they did the Pecos Kid for twenty years for not making any restitution. No one listened to Pecos telling them about how Ira and Ned took it all.

Others couldn't believe those two brave Texas ranchers were rich enough to bid on Gordon's wrecked train.

Gordon's ranch land and livestock were worth a fortune, but who would pay full price for it. Obviously, it came down to Gordon raising sixty thousand dollars to pay off his investors or die in jail.

In his hundred fifty-dollar suit Rose had tailored for him in Dallas, Ira and his partner met in a fancy town house for negotiations.

Ira's first bid for all Samuel's holdings, property, art, furniture, and livestock was thirty thousand.

Samuel's lawyer asked the judge's man was that enough?

The man dismissed it.

Ira offered thirty-five.

That offer was also refused.

Ira and Ned left the room to confer.

"I knew you started too low," Ned said showing a little amusement.

"I am just saving Pecos's money."

They both laughed.

At two o'clock, the judge's man accepted forty thousand for the entire estate to be paid back to his investors.

The host served lunch while the papers were drawn up.

A tired drawn Samuel Gordon sat blank faced all by himself in a hall chair.

Ira stopped beside him. "Do you remember hiring Sanchez to run those homesteaders off your so-called places?"

"No. I had many problems with squatters in those days."

"Listen you hired him to run my family off land opened to homesteading."

He shook his head.

"Those men raped my fifteen-year-old sister and ruined her life. My father later died from his head injury. It broke up our family."

He made a grumpy face at Ira. "Why are you telling me all this crap?"

"I want you to remember this day for the rest of your life. I was nine years old, and those bastards kicked the fire out of me that night. Just remember that the guy did this to you today was that boy that those bastards kicked the hell out of under your orders that night well over a decade ago."

"Screw you."

"No, that goes for you. My wife and I can sleep in your goose down feather bed tonight. And you can freeze your ass off outside."

The papers went through. The agent's men took Samuel to his daughter's house in Dallas, a broken defeated man who would mope the rest of his life away without a silver spoon of his own left to eat off of.

Ira, Rose, Ned, and Jenny enjoyed the estate. Ira began to closely manage that ranch, and in less than two years the profits shot through the roof. In 1872, the foursome were invited guests to be at the presidential inauguration in Washington, D.C.

Inside the White House for one of the occasions, Rose whispered, "Reckon they ever will let a Marble Falls, Texas whore in here?"

"They wouldn't know what that was." He chuckled.

"Did I ever tell you how glad I was you came and got me out of that business?"

"I was pleased to find you."

"We have two kids now. Is that enough?"

"What do you think?" he hugged her shoulders.

"I am the one who always said I was never going to have another. But I love them. I love making them with you. Now, that we have that damn big house, I think we need more."

"When this is over enough for us to slip out, let's go back to the hotel and make another."

She nodded before they shook hands with the first lady and the president of the United States.

EATING TEXAS CROW

THE JULY TEXAS SUN WAS hot when they took the Red River Ferry across the broad, log-choked stream. Ex-Army Sergeant Hayes McBroom and his two pals, still dressed in their tattered Confederate uniforms, stood beside their three nondescript brown horses with Army saddles on the ferry deck. Their trip back took longer from Mississippi because Hayes heard rumors they were giving returning soldiers to Texas a hard time on the eastern border of Texas. Neither he nor his two compadres wanted any trouble from the occupying Yankee forces—the damn war was over. So, they had circled north to avoid any conflict. He wanted to get back to a life he had before the mud and blood of that sorry losing situation called a war.

Randy Darby stood by his horse as the ferry was winched toward the Texas side. Six feet tall like Hayes, his dark curly hair spilled out from under his cap. The lanky twenty-year-old had spoken the same words Hayes felt. *It would be good to be back on Texas soil again.*

There damn sure was no brass band to welcome these three veterans back home that June day. One-eyed Frank Iverson kept bobbing his head, like he couldn't wait to be over there. "It ain't hardly believable. We're getting there, hoss."

Hayes shook his head. "It is even harder after all the hell we saw to imagine we've lived this long."

"We going into Denton today?" Randy asked. "I bet we get cussed out some more by the ones stayed home for us not dying in that damn war."

"Like I said, don't let them rile you. We are former soldiers. We can't afford any trouble with the law. We'll just have to eat lots of that tough Texas crow they're going to feed us."

"We can't simply ride on today either?" Randy asked.

"No, we better rest these horses some and let them graze here. They get weaker by the day, and we're still many miles from the captain's place."

With a scowl on his whiskered face, Frank agreed. "They never were strong horses to start with."

"They've damn sure beat us walking to here," Hayes said to defend them. He hated to think about all the Texan boys who went home barefoot from Mississippi and walked all the way. Glad he wasn't one of them. He noticed a campground of makeshift tents and temporary shelters scattered across the usual grassy area on the south bank. Before the war, this had been a more park-like place under some big walnuts. These were simply lots more war dislocated people with nothing left he guessed.

At last on firm ground, they rode down through the camp. Hayes noticed a young red-headed woman that really caught his eye. He didn't know what it was, but there was something powerfully attractive about her.

Frank pushed in close. "Did you see her?"

"Who was that?"

"The redhead back there. Reckon she's got freckles on her butt?"

"Do you think she'd show them to one of us grubby returning soldiers?"

"Hell, Hayes, you can't tell. I bet you'd suit her."

He shook his head. "Women like that are looking for a real winner. Not one in my class."

"She's probably got a husband big as a gorilla who'd whip your backside, Frank," Randy said.

"If it was after I ate her apple, I might not care."

The three laughed. Hayes noticed there hadn't been anything very funny for them to laugh at lately.

"Let's hobble these ponies to graze, and then we can explore the camp."

"Always the sergeant," Randy said to Hayes. "But we need some of that to survive. You see any of them Yankee soldiers?"

"No. I expected to see some of them here too when we crossed. Maybe they haven't got here yet."

"They told us back there the federal government had their troops out everywhere."

"They can stay the hell home for my part," Frank said.

"They won't," Hayes said, dismounted, and then looked around. "We can camp here. Let's move around and learn what we'll face, if anything, headed for Fort Worth."

His men agreed busy unsaddling their horses.

"Go ahead, Hayes," Frank said. "I'll get your horse. I am going to take a nap."

Hayes agreed and shifted the position of his side arm. "Don't cause any trouble. We need to get south and claim that ranch the captain left us."

Both men agreed, and he set the felt fedora he wore down a little to shade his eyes some more from the glaring sun and started down through the camp.

"Hey, soldier, where are you headed?" a white whiskered man called out.

He shook his head. "I was discharged in Mississippi. I'm a civilian."

"Ha, you're still wearing that uniform."

"I didn't have any other clothes to wear." He wasn't going to argue with a discontented person who acted deeply upset they'd lost. So was he upset over the outcome, but neither of them would change it.

He spoke to another man who was repairing his wagon.

"Where you headed when you get it done?" Hayes asked the man.

"Indian Territory. They say they are going to take over Texas with black soldiers. I don't want to be here and see that."

"I understand. Good luck." Hayes went on down through the camp.

"Mister?" someone called out to him. "Wait."

He stopped and turned to see the flaming red hair and freckled face of the woman he had noticed earlier. She held a nice figure, a little chubby in places, but not fat, it was appealing to him as she carried her wash worn dress hem out of the dirt to catch up to him.

"Good day, sir." She made a small curtsy, and a smile covered her face.

"Same to you."

"My name is Eleanor Hobby, sir. Me and my children need transportation to south Texas."

"Where's your man?"

"I—I have no man. He was shot and killed before the war ended."

"I have no conveyance to move you. Where are you going?"

"I'd hoped to go to San Antonio."

"Do you have kinfolk near there?"

She swept a wave of her hair back. "No."

"Why go there, then?"

"I had hoped to find some kind people there to shelter us. I have two small children, but I am no stranger to hard work. Surely someone can use my skills. I'm willing to do almost anything."

"If I could find a buggy or team, you could go with us. You know it is not safe in these times to be alone with all the lawless things that are going on."

She hugged her arms. "I have no choice but to move on."

"My name is Hayes McBroom. I have a ranch to claim in Bexar County. I know nothing about the facilities I would have for you there."

"I could walk there."

He shook his head. "Your children could not do that."

"I am not going to cry for you to help me. I made it here, and I would promise you anything you would expect of me in trade for a place to live for me and my children."

"I know you are sincere, Eleanor, but to find a conveyance without any money will be hard. Give me a day or two and maybe I can find some way. You have any food?"

"Not much."

"Get your children. My men will move the rest of your things to our camp. You'll be safe there while I look for something."

"I won't disappoint you."

"Fine, get them, and I will take you with us if I find a way."

She acted a little taken back by his offer "God bless you, sir."

Quick like she went to gather her kids and a few things. With a large bag over one arm, she herded the two small ones along toward him.

"Can I carry one?"

She stooped down. "Rachel, can he carry you? It will be a long walk."

Her green eyes studied him, and then the child nodded. Hayes swept her up gently. "I am so glad to meet you, Rachel."

She had no answer for him, but she accepted him while keeping a close watch on her mother and brother to be certain they were not separated. When he reached their camp, he introduced them to the other two, explaining their situation and for them to get her other things while he looked for a conveyance to haul them. They agreed to handle it.

He re-saddled his horse, left his bedroll and rode for town. On the way, he found a small buggy and a piebald welch pony for sale. He stopped and went up on the farmhouse porch to knock on the door.

A woman answered and asked what he wanted.

"I need that buggy you have for sale and pony. A war widow and two children are stranded up here. How much is he asking for it?"

"Twenty dollars."

"If you would trust me. I would send you the money in the coming year."

"He is out at the barn. You better ask him?"

"Thank you. I will go ask him."

He headed around the house and met the man and his stock dog.

"My name's Hayes McBroom. I am going home from the war, sir. There is a widow of a soldier with two children who needs some transportation. I am penniless today, but I have a ranch near Kerrville, and I would send you the money in the next year for the pony and wagon."

The man nodded in agreement. "I believe you would pay me, sir."

"It embarrasses me to not have any money, but I thank you. Will you write down your name and address for me?" He felt like he'd met an honest man.

"Certainly. I feel so sorry we have no money to at least help send you home."

"Thanks for your kind thoughts. It has been trying simply getting here."

The man gave him the paper and helped him hook up the gentle horse. In a short while, he was ready to go, and the man's wife came down and gave him two fresh baked loaves of bread. The yeasty smell went up his nose like manna. The gift shocked him, and he hugged her shoulder in sincere gratitude.

"God bless you both." He hitched his horse behind and drove the pony back to camp.

Frank saw him coming and shouted, "He's found one."

Randy herded her children after her as she went ahead, wringing her hands and looked about to cry. "Oh, he's beautiful."

Hayes stepped down. "He's a dandy. He should get you and the kids to San Antonio."

"What did he cost?" She circled around him in disbelief.

"I owe Mister Dreymeyer twenty dollars."

She peered at him in disbelief and shock. "You bought him on credit?"

"I had nothing to pay him."

She turned and hugged him hard enough so her whole ripe body was pressed to him. Enough he felt embarrassed and couldn't recall that ever happening before "Oh, Hayes, I am so relieved. Thank you."

"I guess we can go on tomorrow. If you want to go with us?"

She stood on her toes and kissed him. A little more at ease with her he wrapped his arms around her and really kissed her back.

"I am so grateful—oh—you are a such a wonderful person. Thank you."

Frank stood by laughing. "We just think he's a good guy too."

"I am sorry, Frank and Randy have been so kind to me today. I was at wits end about what I could do, and you three men have simply solved it."

"We better worry about finding some food. Oh, I have two loaves of fresh bread that his wife sent us."

"Two loaves of fresh bread?" Randy asked. "My God, man, I haven't had any homemade bread in years. Frank, get a sharp knife out. We is going to feast."

Hayes shook his head. "She sent it to be eaten."

"The kids will love it."

"I am sure they will," he said back to her.

So, they all sat on the ground and made a meal out of the bread. It was good to have all they wanted to eat and be satisfied at the end. At home, they'd had butter and maybe some wild fruit jelly, but it still hit the spot.

Sitting cross-legged on the ground, he noted Eleanor had taken a spot close to him. The children went from guy to guy, grinning and eating bread like candy.

"I believe they are having more fun than we are," he said to her.

"Oh, they are. It has been hard on them. I tried to find my late husband's father. They said he was in the Indian Territory. But no one knew of him where I went."

"What was his name?"

"Zen Flock."

"Never heard of him."

"It was a foolish trip."

"You had to do something."

"My only other options were a house of ill repute or starve."

"If you had found him, would he have helped you?"

"I felt since they were his grandchildren he would have. His wife died a few years ago. Things have been so bad in Texas, he hoped to find work up there."

"What do you expect to find in San Antonio?"

"I am not sure. Maybe I can become a housekeeper. But surely, in such a large place, there is work."

"I would hope so. We are going to claim a ranch my captain willed to me. It is above Kerrville."

"I have never been there. But I have heard of it. Do you know what your ranch looks like?"

Hayes shook his head. "He talked about it as being a great ranch. I have no idea, but the three of us have nothing to lose."

"Oh, I hope it is a good one."

"So do we, Eleanor. So do we."

"I was lucky for you to find me today."

"I guess fate put us together. We heard so many bad things happened to soldiers coming in from the east, so we have gone around. Maybe we missed nothing. Now we need to go straight south and find this place of ours."

"Do you expect trouble taking it over?"

"Yes."

"What can they do?"

"Take me to court, tie it up with a judge. Try to scare me off and maybe even shoot me in the back."

"Who? Does he have family?"

"He said he didn't, but claims can come from anywhere."

"What will you need to do to get it?"

"I don't know yet. Maybe when I get there, I can size it up better."

"Sounds tough. I really owe you for today and all you have done for the three of us."

"No, you don't."

"Never mind. I can repay you some day. I need to put my kids to bed."

"Sure. Kiss them for me."

"Oh, I can do that. You've never had a wife?"

"No." He about laughed. No one would have him.

She rose and went to gather the two children up who had been playing with his partners. The little girl kissed Frank and then went off with her brother and momma.

Randy came over. "You all right?"

"I'm fine, anxious to get to the ranch."

"So are we, but she and them won't hurt us."

"No. She's a nice lady. I know nothing more. Time may tell us the rest of her story, or she might. We don't have it all. But I don't fear it. We will let her tag along if she wishes for us to."

"Gawdamn, she's really pretty," Frank said under his breath.

"I won't argue with a one-eyed man. You see it straight," Hayes teased him.

"Damn right I do."

"We have food for tomorrow?" he asked Randy who oversaw that situation.

"We can stretch it for two days."

"We better work on that next."

"We will."

"Good night."

"Yeah, good night."

He went off to his bedroll. Things were quiet in the camp. He noticed how quiet the South had become since the war ended. The surrender took the wind out everyone's sails. No one had an answer for what they'd do next.

He shed his boots and pants and got under the thin blanket for the next morning's coolness. Under his face the small pillow plumped up held him in place on his side.

They were still a week or more short of San Antonio. What did the future hold for him?

––––––––––––––

"DON'T BE SPOOKED. IT'S ME." Her soft words in his ear shocked him. "I have really been a problem for you to solve today." She was under his cover, and he quickly realized the silky shift she wore was very skimpy.

She continued, "We're adults. What we do is our business. I did not come to shock you. I wish to see if I could please you."

"What if I do not please you," he whispered in her ear.

She shook her head, and he saw the smile in the starlight before he kissed her.

"I have one more thing. If I make love to you tonight, and you like it, will you marry me?" he asked her.

"You don't have to marry me."

"I don't have to make love to you either. If you like it, will you marry me?"

She closed her eyelids. "I came to repay you, not to trap you."

"What do you say?"

"Yes, I will if you never ever say that I trapped you."

Gentle like he pushed the thin gown up to expose more of her smooth skin. "I so promise."

She kissed him hard, and they were both swept away.

He awoke by himself the next morning before the sun came up. Where had his bride to be gone? Had he only dreamed she came and did that—no, his recollection was too defined of their lovemaking. The mole he found secreted on her body. That was no dream. Now, on top of it all, he had a wedding to plan for.

He dressed and joined Randy building a fire. He squatted down beside him. "All is going well?"

"We will have food ready in a short while. Oatmeal. I borrowed some sugar last night from a lady for the children. Grownups can swallow it, but I couldn't let those little kids have to do that."

"You're sure some tough veteran giving little kids sugar." He clapped him on the shoulder and rose up at the sight of her. "Keep working on it."

"Good morning, Eleanor."

"Good morning, Hayes. Tell him hi, kids."

"Hi," her sleepy little boy said, while the little girl buried her face in her mother's dress.

"She's not talking yet. Too early."

"I savvy. I don't talk, 'fore I get my morning coffee, either. We have oatmeal. Randy borrowed some sugar for theirs, thank him."

"I sure will. What else?"

"Do you want to back out of our pact?"

She shook her head. "Do you?"

He shook his head, and they both laughed.

Shortly they were through eating and on the road. The three riders went ahead and the spotted pony and her brought up the rear. But he was not a lazy horse. He stepped out and was right behind them all day. They took some breaks and found a grassy place to camp that evening. They passed the pony's former home that morning, but he never slacked. By the end of the day, Hayes felt he had made a wonderful buy.

Eleanor agreed and tried to walk the stiffness out of her body while the men played with the children in their camp. Two fat hens were waiting to be silenced and their feathers plucked for supper, Randy bought them for twenty cents from a farm boy. But Frank said he wondered if they were the boy's to sell even, but they ate roasted chicken and smiled. Oatmeal was planned for the next morning, and with the kids asleep, the two of them went off for a walk and to visit.

"I'll be so glad when we have some money to buy food and essentials." Hayes shook his head in disappointment.

"You and your friends are quite successful finding food."

He looked at the twinkling stars. "I promise you will not have to live hand to mouth when we get settled."

"Oh, Hayes, I believe you. I thanked God last night for sending you to me. I know when we get settled that things will be much better. Don't apologize. You are a great giver in my eyes."

"Has all of Texas been like this during the war?"

"Without a garden you could have starved. There is less money in Texas now than there was before the war. They have no gold like California has. Things have been very, very desperate for everyone."

"I hope we can make this ranch work. I have dreamed all my life of having a large ranch. The captain said I could have his if he was killed. We didn't want him killed. He made out the will to me. Another officer, a lawyer, wrote it for him and said it was legal and registered by the seal on it."

"Are you excited about it?"

"Having you or having the ranch?"

"I'm not much."

"Yes, you are. I am very excited about you agreeing to marry me. I simply want it to go better getting you there so I can."

"I'm not worried about you succeeding. You will find a way."

"We are still several days from even San Antonio—"

She bent him down and whispered in his ear, "Go back to bed, and when they are asleep, I will join you, and I can make you stop worrying."

He closed his eyes. "Oh, Eleanor, I love you so much."

They kissed and went back. His partners were asleep. She let him get in his blankets, then she partial undressed to join him. She made him forget everything, then kissed him and returned to her own bedroll.

The next day, they were on the road and heard shots. He told her to stay back and the three rode ahead to better see what was happening. Half hidden by post oak trees where the road dipped in a draw, he made out two flour sack masked men who were robbing two others dressed in suits. There was a blue veil of gun smoke in the trees from the shots they heard, but when they reined up their horses on the high spot they could see it all. A robbery holdup was in progress.

They drew their pistols and charged off the hill. At the first shot one of the flour sacked men jerked around, but their vision must have been reduced by their masks, and they shot wildly at the three. The ex-soldiers could shoot better, and the would-be robbers soon were shot off their horses. The two businessmen in suits still had their hands raised like they thought Hayes and his men were only some more holdup men.

Frank told them to put them down, they weren't outlaws, just soldiers going home. Hayes had the youngest outlaw jerked up by the shirt collar. He was bleeding all over.

"Who the hell are you?"

"Joe. Green."

"What's his name?"

"Chuckaluck Jones."

Jones wasn't breathing. He grabbed Green's Bowie knife out of his sheath and discarded it. Then he let the desperado fall back on the ground. "You men all right? They about had you two robbed. Ever seen them before?"

Both well-dressed men were white faced as paste. Even noticeably shaking when Eleanor drove up.

"No," the younger man managed to say.

"You three saved our lives. My name is Ted Rhodes, and this is my partner Charles Hatton. We own the National Bank of Texas in Austin."

"My name is Hayes McBroom. I own the XYZ. We'll be at the XYZ ranch near Kerrville. We're on our way home. That is my fiancée, Eleanor. Meet Frank and Randy, they are my Army pals."

"I can see you have traveled long and hard. Would a hundred dollars be enough to pay you and your men for saving our lives?" Rhodes asked him.

He heard Eleanor swallow hard. At that point, he put his arm on Rhodes shoulder and walked him a few feet away. "Now, that other outlaw, he won't see more than a few days in jail and some attorney will have him out. But for two hundred dollars we will take him down this draw and let Judge Tree carry out his execution for the crime."

Rhodes drew a thick wallet, licked his thumb and counted out three U.S. brand new Yankee one hundred dollar bills he handed to him. "My bank is in Austin. You ever need any money, come see me. That is exactly how I wanted it handled."

Frank and Randy had the bankers horses caught when they came back and held them while the two well-dressed men mounted them.

"But Charles what about the live one?" Ted asked.

"Ted, I have that matter taken care of. Nice to meet you, ma'am, and you men. Thanks again." They rode off.

"Eleanor, take the pony and children up on the hill." He lowered his voice, "I agreed with them to lynch this last outlaw. We will only be a short while, and we will meet you up there."

She looked pale faced and swallowed, and he helped her in the rig with the excited children. Her on the seat, he turned to Frank. "Go with her while we clean up. We won't be long."

"Sure. Sure. You don't need me?" Frank asked.

"I'll be fine, Hayes," she said to protest his concern about her.

"Go with her, Frank." They rode off together.

He turned to Randy. "I told them we'd lynch him. Ain't no law here now. He'd get off anyway."

Solemn faced, Randy agreed.

They made a noose, threw it over a tree limb, tied his hands behind his back and stuck the dying outlaw in the saddle. Fastened the noose on his neck, Hayes slapped the horse on the rump hard to get him to bolt away. Green danced on the rope some and then went limp.

He and Randy picked up their guns and decided that their horses were not worth being recognized, so they left them loose and drug the corpse off in the weeds still wearing his flour sack mask.

In the saddle, Randy looked all around to be sure they had it all before he asked, "Did he pay you a hundred dollars?"

"No."

Randy frowned, trying hard not to grind his teeth together. "Damn, I thought he'd pay you something."

"I asked for two hundred to lynch that last one, he thought that was above the hundred he owed us and paid us three hundred dollars."

"Holy Cow. Why that was highway robbery?"

Laughing, they began to lope their horse to catch up.

"No, he had hundreds more in that wallet."

"Them two outlaws knew what they were doing didn't they?"

"Like most criminal minds they simply didn't know how to do it and not get caught."

"Right."

So that night in the next small town they stayed in two hotel rooms after a fine supper in the café. He had a hot bath drawn for her and him in the room after the kids were asleep on a pallet. She even shaved his six weeks of whiskers off him. The evening passed pleasantly.

"Well, I must finally ask you. He must have paid you the hundred dollars?"

"We cleaned up the mess, and he added two hundred more."

She laughed aloud. "See I told you that you would figure this out. Now, turn out the light. I am going to do my part."

He squeezed her tight and kissed her. She was the best part of the whole deal.

But while he slept, he again saw the outlaw Green dancing his last with his boots off the ground again. That was the worst part of the whole thing for him.

THE NEXT DAY THEY REACHED the outskirts of Fort Worth. He traded the pony and cart, for a Morgan mare and a light two-seat carriage with a top shade for thirty dollars and the pony outfit. They rode on and made it uneventfully to San Antonio in five more days.

With her and the children in a hotel room, the three veterans went to the county land office. A clerk at the county land office told Hayes a lawyer would have to present it to a judge and get a decision rendered. He checked around and found who they told him was a reasonable lawyer.

John Edwards saw the three in his office and explained he could get it settled for thirty dollars. How could they pay him?"

"When you can get the deed in mine and my wife's name and registered, I will pay you that in cash."

"Yes, sir. I'll get on it right now. Last rancher I did this for paid me in calves."

"I have the money."

"Good, meet me at the courthouse at two p.m. tomorrow. We can have it registered then."

"The brand, too?"

"The brand also."

"We will meet you there then."

"What now?" Randy asked when they were out in the sunshine.

"I need a justice of the peace. And I need to find her a new dress to get married in. You two can be my witness and hold the kids."

"One thing I like about him," Randy said.

"What's that?" Frank asked.

"He damn sure don't mess around getting things done."

The frilly dress cost him eight dollars, and the hat cost two. The outfit made her cry. The JP married them close to four p.m., and they rode back to the hotel in her carriage. Both of his men planned to meet them for breakfast at the square across from the Alamo.

Amused, he wondered how many newly married couples carried their two kids up to the second floor of the hotel on their wedding night. He loved them already, though, and he was real close to having the ranch deal settled. After all those lousy days as a soldier in the war, his life was finally going to open up.

He wondered what day her birthday fell on. She wrote in seventeen as her age on the certificate. *Robbing the cradle.* Her son was three. No four.

The kids asleep and their love making over, he squeezed her hand. "Tell me the truth. I really want to know. How old were you when you first got married?"

"Twelve."

"Wasn't that young?"

She snuggled up against him. "I didn't think so. At the time, I wanted him as bad as I wanted you that day when I first saw you up at the Red River when you rode by. I am not some floozy. I have been in bed with two men in my life. Him and you."

"I don't doubt you. I simply never considered marrying a twelve-year-old girl."

"Didn't bother him. It didn't bother me back then, but I know now, we'd have always been poor as dirt. He didn't have your mind. It takes brains to make money and run a business. You have them. And you came down here, and found that lawyer, Edwards. Day after tomorrow we drive to your new ranch. Take two days?"

"Yeah. We can talk about that tomorrow."

She went to chuckling. "I know you want some more of my ranch tonight."

"Does that bother you?"

"Why no. I am just proud you want me period. Two kids for baggage and I'm an old used woman."

"Don't say that. You're my doll, and I love you."

"Tell me that in seven months when I am big as a barrel."

"Seven months?"

"It may be longer than that, but I doubt it. You rub sticks together, you get fire. We've been really rubbing things together."

"You will still be my doll."

"We will see. Love me now. I promise to shut up."

Twenty-four hours later, his ranch and brand ownership were recorded. The captain had paid the last year's taxes before he was killed. Hayes owed forty-seven dollars the first of the year on them. He decided it must be a great ranch with that much tax on it.

Edwards said one more thing to him before they parted. He was going to check on all the banks to see if the captain had any money on deposit. He would use the last will to include any of the bank accounts the captain may have left. Edwards said, so far, he had not found any, but if there was any chance, he would get ten percent of the find. They shook on that.

It took two days for them to reach Kerrville. They stayed in a hotel that night. The next day they drove up the long valley on a map that a bartender drew the night before for Randy. Smoke was coming out of the chimney of the main house when they stopped to get a good distant view of the place.

"Who lives there?" Randy asked.

"Cap'n left some *vaqueros* in charge, he told me. Must be them."

"Hold up. Hayes, you think that they will buck us?" Randy asked.

"No."

Randy stopped her. "Eleanor, when we get closer, you stop that little mare and wait. We may have some fireworks up here."

"I will, Randy. Thank you."

The three men advanced on the adobe jacals and corrals. There was a large, fenced field on the right with the corn about waist high. The fencing around it was smooth wire, stays and posts like many used for containing goats and sheep.

When they approached the main house, a Mexican woman came out and looked them over with her hand shielding the bright sun from her eyes.

Hayes spoke to her in fluent Spanish. "Good day, *señora*. My name is Hayes McBroom."

She nodded. "*Señor*, we have wondered when you would come."

Her words shocked him. "He wrote and told you I would be coming?"

"*Si.* He told us in a letter, if he did not come back, that you would. Welcome to the *ranchero*, and is that your wife and children?"

"Yes. She is Eleanor." He turned in the saddle, then stopped. "What is your name *señora?*"

"Lupe Montez."

"Eleanor, this Lupe Montez."

She reined up the mare, climbed down and unloaded the children. "I am so glad to meet you, Lupe. This is Sam and that is Rachel."

"Come let us go around in the shade."

"Lupe, that is Randy and this here is Frank."

She bowed to them. "So nice you all came."

"So nice you were here to greet us." He noticed other women and children that came on the run as if beckoned to come to meet the new party. Skirt in their hands and herding youngsters, he soon met three more wives.

"How many men work here?"

"My husband, Don, and these women's men."

"How have you eaten all these years?"

"He left us some money, and we raise many things. Texas is a poor land. But we had roofs over our heads. The land is very tillable, so we stayed. He asked us to protect his cattle and to brand more. The men have done that. They have many head of wild cattle branded."

"Did he say what he would do with them?"

She smiled. "He said some day there will be a market for them."

"I wonder where he meant for that to happen?"

Lupe shook her head. She didn't know. "Tonight, we can move our things from the *casa*."

"No, we can sleep somewhere. We are not fancy people. You stay in there,"

"Yes. Yes," Eleanor said. "We have slept on the ground so long to get here. A hammock would be fine."

"I can tell you are not the people we were so concerned about coming. *Gracias*."

"Frank and I will put up the horses and acquaint ourselves. Are the men coming back tonight?" Randy asked her.

"Oh, *si, señor* They are out working the cattle today. I have some cool tea. Come back when you get through. What part of Texas did you use to live at?" she asked Hayes.

"Up by Fort Worth. My men lived east of that."

"How long have you been married?"

"A few days."

Her brown eyes flew open. "I thought—"

"We met a few weeks ago. Her husband died in the war. She had no one, and like you say, things are tough. We got married in San Antonio."

"Oh my, you are newlyweds."

"Don't fuss over us. We are happy, and now we want to make this ranch work."

"Will you need us?"

"Oh, yes. Payrolls may be hard to make, but we will figure it out. Someday things will be better. I will need all of you."

"Ladies, ladies, the patron says we can stay and work."

They cheered.

"I think they were more worried than we were," Eleanor said, swinging on his arm. "The children are very tired. I am going to put them down somewhere."

"Take them in my *casa*. Two of us will get the tea. There is a pallet there for them."

Eleanor thanked her and herded her brood in the house. The men sat on benches under the cottonwood trees that rattled with the warm wind, and the hardworking windmill creaked a little pumping water out the iron pipe.

His ranch surprised him some. He had a working force attached to the land, and they worked wild cattle. His next job was to find a market for those cattle.

Hell, if he had that done, the source of market would be overrun that night by the rest of Texas. He had lots to learn. But these men had been working. If the rainfall continued, the corn crop would be valuable. They had several acres of it. He bet they had more land in *frijoles*. Staples they could eat. Money that did not grow on bushes would be hard to get his hands on, but he would not be alone. Besides, the Confederate money that most folks held was worthless.

Her tea was cool and very refreshing. The men thanked her. It felt good to simply have a little time to sit after their long push. Their acceptance made that easier too. He had held all kinds of wild fears about obtaining this ranch. They had all evaporated in ten minutes. The things he worried about the most lifted like a fog, but now, how to get the money to run it bothered him.

Lupe organized the women, sending them off in many directions for different things. Randy offered to help and so did Frank, but she told them that they could handle it. Some thunderheads gathered as the day slipped by and the women were busy cooking some beef. Eleanor visited with them, asking questions and making them laugh.

When the thunder roared close by. They strung tarps with ropes to trees to roof their operation. They acted unperturbed that rain might ruin their event. It was the border way, Hayes decided. The leading cool wind swept up some dust, but the first hard downpour dropped the temperature twenty degrees. The rain which followed was softer and the storm growled around them. It was a great rain, and he thanked God for the blessing he'd sent him.

The ranchmen returned wearing canvas raincoats. Hayes and his friends shook their hands with Lupe's introductions and told them how glad they were to meet them. The oldest was Lupe's husband, Don, then Romero, Benito and Pancho, the youngest man.

"Did your day go well?"

"Oh, *si, señor*. We worked twenty-five head today."

"That was a good day. How many cattle do we have?"

"Over two thousand."

"Steers, cows, heifers, and bulls?"

"He said to brand them all. We could not have too many cattle."

"You have worked hard to get that much done."

"Some days I have wondered why?"

"No. No, I feel he knew something we don't know, but I am going to find out. Your farming is excellent. We will all eat this winter. Money for your work will be hard to find."

"*Señor*, we have no place to go better than here. We can, like you say, eat here, that is more important than money today. Texas will not always be so poor. I say war hurt us, but that, too, will pass."

"Getting there will be tough."

"*Señor*, life has no easy path."

"You're right."

So, a routine began. They moved Eleanor and Hayes into a cleaned adobe casa. It was the last one in the row and more private, Lupe said with a smile.

They ate the meals community style at the tables. The women had them food ready, they ate, and then the *vaqueros* saddled up to ride out. His two men went along to learn the trade. He decided to see about the town and business in general. His pockets were down to less than twenty dollars, but he promised Lupe to buy some Arbuckle Coffee if any could be had.

In the mercantile, he found that many shelves were empty. They had no coffee except some Mexican coffee beans that must be roasted and ground. He bought and paid for two dollars' worth. That was a sizeable cloth sack of it.

The owner came out and shook his hand. His name was Goldstein. Ira was his first name. A man behind square glasses acted very friendly toward him. "Don and I have talked about exchanging corn this fall for staples like flour and sugar."

Hayes agreed. "I am certain those are good plans. We make corn, you will have our business."

"I have absolutely no idea what these occupation forces will do to us, but it won't be good."

"I think I was lucky about clearing my title before they really got things in their hands."

"I think you were, too. Maybe they will get tired and go back north."

"No, they say 'to the victors go the spoils.' They will have mined all of Texas worth before they leave."

In the Lone Star Saloon down by the Portales River, he heard rumors that Texas cattle at the Missouri rail head would bring twenty to thirty dollars a head in Yankee money. Many folks were trying to gather cattle and to go up there with them since the surrender had been signed. He could hardly believe that such a place or market even existed and shook his head. They must be smoking Chinese pipes.

He rode home with a sack of hard candy for the children and her coffee, wondering the whole way, how many miles that place in Missouri was from Kerrville. The name of the Missouri town came and went into his busy mind. He finally recalled it, Sedalia, Missouri, was the town where the tracks ended up there.

John Cosby, a man in his forties, came by one day to meet and talk to him. He wore a suit that had seen better days and a white shirt with a raveled worn-out collar. No tie, his felt hat was weathered and storm beaten, but the man still had lots of pride. Hayes liked that in any man.

"How many cattle could you spare me? I need five hundred head at least to go up there and cover my expenses. I can't guarantee I can even sell them when I get there. But depending on if I do, each steer you send with me is a share which, after I pay my expenses, will be the divider that I use on repayment. How many cattle would you risk with me?"

"Say you get some more. I'll send two hundred head along."

"Oh, God bless you, sir."

"I don't know about that, John. But I will have to pray hard while you are gone to make it."

"Yes, God willing. Would you send another hundred head if I get more?"

"Get your herd, and yes, I would send that many with you if you need them."

"May God bless you, Hayes. I plan to leave in two weeks. Now I need to get more cattle committed."

When John Cosby left that afternoon, she came over and rubbed his stiff shoulders while he sat on the small wooden barrel. "What does your crystal ball say now?"

"If he gets me ten buck a head. I will be a lot richer than I am now."

"Three hundred head would bring three thousand dollars. I would say so. What are you going to do now?"

"Ride out and tell the men to round up three hundred big steers." He swept her up in his arms and kissed her hard. "We better pray a lot for that man making it up there. He ain't no kid. But he just may get there with them."

She agreed. "I hope so, 'cause I want you to stop worrying about money."

He squeezed her tight against him. "I'd probably worry how to make some more, but wouldn't that be fun to have that kind of money?"

"I hope he makes it."

"So do I, darling. So do I."

The next five days they sorted and gathered three hundred and five steers. John Cosby sent word to Hayes that with his three hundred and the rest John'd signed on, he'd drive a thousand head north."

The cattle were road branded and delivered to his place north of Kerrville. Hayes shook John's hand that day and wished him all the luck in the world, and then they rode back to wait and wait some more all summer.

The corn made over fifty bushels per acre by his estimate and everyone helped shock it to dry. When it was dry, then they'd shucked it and stacked the stalks for winter cow feed. Mr. Goldstein said they had the best corn in the country when he drove by one day and was excited talking about forty cents a bushel. Hayes hoped it brought fifty cents. Then they harvested the *frijoles*, and everyone worked at it. By counting even some of the children, he had a great labor force. Bean gathering also proved a big chore, but the results were fantastic.

"Next year, we plant our corn in the bean field and beans over there," Don told him.

"Why is that?" Hayes asked him.

"The captain told me the beans help the soil. It really works. We have had some good yields doing that. He knew many things."

"I wish he was here now."

"He was a great man and trusted us."

He clapped Don on the back that was pulling up more bean pod loaded plants to toss on the wagon. "Anyone who knew you would trust you."

The women sorted out the beans in a large dry barn. The bean plants would feed the milk cows in the winter. Nothing was thrown away. Tomatoes were sliced and dried on racks for later usage. The summer passed, and they prepared land to plant oats for winter forage and later hay. No word from John Cosby came, then in October, word came he was coming home and had sold the cattle in Sedalia for cash. It was a telegram John's wife shared with the group of his cattle donors that he sent her from up at Denton. Still two weeks went by, but everyone's spirits were up looking forward to some kind of payday anyhow.

He heard many of the reluctant ones say they wished they'd sent their cattle with him. Hayes was truly glad John talked him into putting three hundred head in the drive.

When he took Goldstein some of the first shucked corn, a neighbor stopped him. "How many head did you send with Crosby anyway?"

"Three hundred head. Why?" Hayes paused and looked at the man,

"Why word is, when he finally got there, he topped the market."

"Sounds good to me. You send any?"

"Naw, I never figured he'd get through to there and still be alive."

"I knew it wouldn't be any Sunday School picnic."

"Even if I don't have any money coming, I want to hear his story."

Hayes agreed. "I bet he has a good one."

When word came that Crosby reached San Antonio, they began to gather up a party to celebrate his arrival. But before he arrived the occupation forces sent a company of forty black soldiers to Kerrville to stop the plans for any form of public celebration. The white officer in charge of them read the order out loud that Texas was under lock and key by the federal forces and no public celebrations were allowed by order of the general in charge. Any such occasion would be seen as treason by the attendees and was to be prohibited by force. Forty black soldiers with bayonets put teeth in the order.

Hayes stood on the front porch of Goldstein's store and listened to the man's loud lecture to the grown children of Texas. Before this occupation was over, the state of Texas under the pressing federal thumb, the residents would eat a whole lot of tough crow.

JOHN CROSBY, THE HERO OF the day, came to his ranch two days later. He had two hard-eyed rannies on horseback for guards along with him, and they carried shotguns across their laps. When Crosby took off his hat for Eleanor, she escorted him to the big table with everyone gathered around—the poor man looked to Hayes like he had aged ten years.

He shook every man's hand and then sat down.

"Boys, I'm glad I went. I saved five ranches, besides my own. But Texas longhorns have tick fever and when a tick from one of them crawls on an Ozark milk cow, she dies. They wanted to hang us for that. There are rocks up there called flint rocks in those mountains that can cripple a steer in three miles travel. We were shot at and threatened all the way up there, and I hired armed guards to get back here.

"It damn sure was worth it. But I ain't going back there ever again. I may take cattle north but not through them Ozarks."

"John, I noticed you have aged a bit, but tell us what we made."

"After expenses. I'll pay you about twelve thousand Yankee greenbacks."

Hayes couldn't believe him. "That's forty bucks a head."

"They sold for forty-eight dollars apiece. I couldn't believe it myself. I was barricaded in a railroad office. All my men armed with repeating rifles guarding me and that was the highest bid. We lost a few but not many, and you plus four other families made a killing. But I swear to God, boys, that was the toughest time in my entire life."

"John, I hope you took enough out to pay all your bills. We thank you. These four men and their families here have worked this ranch for three years without pay. I will pay them today. I know the Yankees said no celebrations in Kerrville, but we have one planned for you here today. We have a milk fat calf we butchered and cooked all night. There are plenty of fixings. Frank, you say grace, and we will eat."

"I can't believe that bunch in Austin did that," Crosby said. "Crazy business, no celebrations. Why we ain't going to jump on their asses."

"John, that is only a pin head of things I see in our future. They plan to make Texas eat crow on their hands and knees before they are through with us, if ever?"

"Hayes, it makes me sick to hear you say that. But I think this cattle business is going to really help Texas. I think if we can get linked to markets and a better way to get them up there, we will all prosper."

"It may be the only way we can get off our knees. You ever need anything, you call on me."

The music began. Guitars played, and fiddles sawed a song, and they ate and danced. After that, John went on to his next stop. Hayes gave each man three hundred dollars and that included his two partners who wanted to decline it. No, they'd earned it getting him there.

Every one of the workers wives came by and kissed him. The wine flowed, and he and his bride danced round and round. Lupe took their two children at the end to her casa and told them to keep celebrating. They did, and in the middle of all the fun and pleasure, his wife asked him, "What do you have to worry about now?"

"I guess about getting you pregnant."

She hugged him, "That's over. I am."

"My God, that is wonderful."

"We will see how wonderful it is. But I am happy for you and the new one we have coming."

He mailed the pony seller thirty dollars the next time he went into town. Then he placed a two-hundred-dollar grocery order for the ranch cooks at Goldstein's Store which included Arbuckle Coffee, raisins, sugar, canned peaches, wheat flour, baking powder, spices, cinnamon, dried apples, and a dozen more things he didn't even have in stock.

Goldstein came out of his office and took him into a corner. "I need to make a thousand-dollar order for the store to restock the shelves. I can pay you back with twenty percent interest in one year."

"What does a bank charge?"

"Thirty-five percent."

"That is high. When do you need it?"

"This week."

"I will come back tomorrow and loan it to you."

"I will be grateful."

"Find my cooks some Arbuckle coffee. I ordered some today, but you have none."

"I will do that too."

The big Jewish man would repay him. He had no doubt, but he also saw the power of money in a tight economy. Money really talked.

After that sale of cattle, money had proved so good Don told him they needed to change their ranching operation to strictly catching steers. That was where the money was at, and Hayes agreed.

Fall winds swept out of the north. Cottonwoods turned gold but the temperature remained much milder down there than the winters he had felt as a boy in north Texas. The oats got rain and were doing good.

The ranch women ordered Mason jars and a cooker for the next year. Goldstein found them a bargain, and they had scads of shiny jars to use. The next season they'd have lots of them full of safe to eat food.

Randy met a sister to one of the wives on the ranch named Carla, and the two of them came to him wanting to get married.

"Go get married," he told them.

"Where will we live?"

"In a new house we can build. When does it need to be ready?"

"Could we move in around Christmas?"

"I will try." He called the whole crew in the next day and told them his plans.

Don set in to tell them what they each must do next. It was like planting oats, they fell in, worked the ground, sowed oats, and someone harrowed them in. The house came up the same way, supplies ordered, piers made, hammers rang. and the cedar shingles split by a Mexican were nailed all on in three weeks.

They didn't miss much cattle gathering either.

A salesman came by with a sheet advertising Abilene, Kansas, as the new market west of the Kansas tick deadline with a railroad siding and many buyers.

That evening he rode over and talked to John about it.

"Sounds good. I talked to some others who been up there, and besides all the rivers to cross it is all pretty much open grassland," Crosby said.

"If I could follow you, I'd take a herd up there. My boys say we could gather a thousand head of our own."

"That might be the thing to do, but getting help won't be easy. None of the married men wanted to leave their wives for that long. They fear they'll lose their place in bed, I guess. Help will be the hard thing. I also heard that Charlie Goodnight, an ex-Ranger, built a wagon to be his kitchen and pantry and took it to Kansas last year. That would sure beat the hell out of packing all of it on horses or mules."

"I thought so too."

"Where can we see one? My men can build houses, they can fix one of them up," Hayes said.

"I reckon up at Fort Worth. There may be some in San Antonio."

"I want to go see one. I may take the buggy and Don, my foreman, in there to see if we can find one. He can build it."

"Let me know. You can follow us next spring. Just so we don't mix herds. My boy is talking about riding up there this winter."

"I can tell you what. He better dress warm. The snow blows around up there this time of year." Hayes knew it got cold up there.

"I'll tell him what you said." Crosby laughed. "He may not want his manhood froze off."

"It can happen up there for sure in the wintertime."

He and Don went to San Antonio the next week. They left Randy in charge and took some fast ranch horses. They found five chuck wagons as they called them being built in various blacksmith shops. While Hayes talked to the shop man or owner of the business at each stop. Don prowled the actual work in progress and of course Hayes learned why each man had a better idea on what to put in one. Most of the conversions of the original ambulances cost up to five hundred dollars. Later, Don told him on the side that gold plated hardware on the cabinets was unnecessary.

They bought a near new wagon and a pair of Belgian cross black mules to pull it. Purchased cabinet grade oak lumber and the brass hardware, hickory wagon bows, and the canvas to cover it for three hundred dollars.

Cash money talked Hayes learned fast in the San Antonio market. Several people asked him if he had been one of the lucky ones to get his cattle sold in Missouri. He gave a nod and few details. There were posters all over between there and his ranch advertising Abilene, Kansas, as the new shipping point. He worried how crowded by early summer the road north that the poster described would be choked with bawling cattle.

Christmas was an important time. And this year, they even had money to spend on that event. Eleanor was coaching Juanita for her wedding to Randy, shortly before the holiday. Of course, Randy had the money to buy her a wedding dress, and the ranch was footing the bill for the celebration.

A cooler time of year, even in south Texas, the ranch women worried about rain that Saturday. Hayes found a circus tent in San Antonio. And for fifty dollars they brought it out there and set it up for the event.

Frank asked him. "How much will that cost?"

"Fifty dollars," Hayes told him. "Those men have no money either, plus I have to feed them several days."

Don's chuck wagon project was drawing the curious. He found a master cabinet man in Mason who built the chuck box, made all the things they wanted like water barrel mounts on both sides, and he made some iron rings on the sides of the box that were reinforced to strap logs on the side to float it across rivers if they ever needed to do that. Women sewed and beeswaxed the seams on the canvas topper with reinforced pieces for tie down ropes and hooks made in the blacksmith shop to tie it down.

"You think this gun boat will be better than pack horses?" Jud Stone, a big-time rancher from the west, asked them. Stone had only sent a hundred head with Crosby and grumbled about his own stingy ways for not sending more.

"You can hire a cook to use this is the way I figure. Punching cattle all day is a tiresome deal, and a good chow line will keep them going."

"Aw hell, I'm going to be paying them fifteen dollars a month. That should be good enough."

Hayes bit his tongue. Stone had not learned what John found out about who they could hire. Bad financial times or not, real good hands would be hard to find. A thousand head herd could bring the seller as much as fifty thousand dollars. He wasn't going to risk that much money on it being done by fifteen dollars-a-month hands.

The word was out in the area, if you wanted to go north with a sharp outfit, you had better get your bid in with the XYZ ranch and to see Don or Hayes.

Men and boys drifted in. Some did not appear to be tough enough to suit Hayes. No telling what outlaws would try on them along the way. A man that could shoot a pistol or rifle was one requirement. He brought home sacks of brown bottles from town for practice and testing that they set up in a dry wash to save stock and people from being shot by their stray bullets.

Goldstein began to buy up rifles for his trip, most were lever action, some which took tubes of fifty-six caliber rim fire cartridges. They were Spencer's. He also had some "yellow boy's" from Winchester in .44 caliber. The rifle's works were brass and many thought after much usage the guns would be worn out. New, they weren't any problem, but an argument went on about preferences. Hayes and Goldstein both were concerned that their arms buying might put them under the scrutiny of the Army. They did not need that either, so the merchant made small purchases of bullets, gunpowder, and lead.

There were a lot of different pistols around, all they had were cap and ball. Most in .44 or .36 caliber. Both the Army and Navy model Colts were really made by Belgian Arms as duplicates for the Confederacy to use. At first, it sounded like the occupational officials wanted all the Texans disarmed, but no way could one exist in the Lone Star State unarmed between the vicious Comanche and the bad guys—firearms were a necessity for survival. Disbanding rangers was another bad deal for folks like Hayes that lived on the western frontier and the dismissals of rangers encouraged more Indian raids and open outlaws.

Hayes sought others who went north the last year, but they all said the Ozarks route was impossible and maybe the rails had been extended to southwest Missouri. No one knew a thing about that. He finally decided he'd simply follow Crosby using Joe McCoy's route to Abilene. The refurbished chuck wagon was the finest he had seen and well-reinforced to stand lots of bumps he knew it must take on the ungraded trail north.

Hayes went over the horses for soundness. He knew well the old adage about the war was lost for lack of one horse. That made him tough on horses with weaknesses who might give out on the trail. His plans were to take seven horses per cowboy. That meant the horses only had to work one of seven days and could regain their strength on grass and no grain would be needed to supplement them.

Don agreed to manage the ranch, so Hayes, Randy, and Frank could all go north plus eight drovers to help them. Crosby was right—married men turned down his offer to work for him, despite the fact that Hayes knew that none of them had a pot to piss in. Still, not a one of them he wanted would go to work on the drive.

Don made a trip to old Mexico and came back with nine *vaqueros.* They were all less than thirty years old and real horsemen. After Hayes met and talked to them, they all said they really needed the work. There was none in Mexico, and they were willing to spend six to eight months on the trail driving cattle with a long ride back home.

Hayes felt satisfied these men would be loyal. They were in an unknown land, and they were not good at English. Farther north, less white men would speak Spanish to them. But they were stockmen and rode like pros. On good horses, they should be all the hands he needed to get his cattle up the trail.

At night in bed, Eleanor and he talked about his venture.

"I hate leaving you the most. The baby's coming, and I will be gone."

"Oh, Hayes, I have had two children already, and I am hardy. I have even grown stronger since I became your wife. Have you noticed?"

"Yes. I have noticed you every day since the first night. You are one of the best things in my life. I look forward each day to our lovemaking, and I won't have you to talk to either. The captain leaving me this ranch was a great opportunity to set us up in life. Our cattle sales last year were a lucky windfall. But we may beat all that and get to expand the XYZ next year with this trip.

"I agree. And I know what you want to do, and I love you for it and for being so easy on me. I worried when I told you I would marry you if I could ever please you because you expected so much of yourself and everything you do."

"Silly girl, I was so pleased you agreed to my terms, you could never disappoint me."

"When you return, I want a house of my own on your list. Not next year, but in the future, down the road. Three children won't crowd us immediately, but who knows, there might be more after this one."

He tickled her, and she laughed. "I will be fine, but hurry home."

"Don and Lupe will care for you and the kids. And I will be riding home this fall."

"The ranch hands are so grateful for all you've done here."

"I told Goldstein that if he needed more money, you would furnish it."

"I can do that. His business is really growing isn't it?"

"Some money is seeping into the state. It filters down but we've got a helluva long ways to go."

She arched her back and raised her sleeping gown up under the light covers to expose herself. "Now let's make love. You haven't left me yet."

"Yes, I wondered when you'd ask?"

She poked him hard in the side of his rock-hard belly. "I am always ready for you to do anything you wish to me. Love me hard. I will postpone missing you for another night."

They kissed and savored each other's skin against their own. This was the greatest woman in the world in his arms. No one could have fit the role better than this flaming red head he found north of Denton coming home.

The next day he rode over to Crosby's place to talk more about their preparations and things he felt were necessary to have along. John had a wife. He wondered if she wasn't older than him by ten years. Gray headed, she had the nose and dark complexion of a part Indian, a thin woman with hawk eyes. No children running around, Maude met him at the door to their log house.

"He's down by the corral." Then she stepped outside over the log threshold in her wash-worn dress and pointed to the corral.

"Thanks, Maude."

"No thanks about it. That's where he is."

"I'll find him," he said and turned his horse southward. Someday Crosby would tell him about her. He wanted to hear that story.

"Tell him not to be late for his dinner. He hates cold food."

"I will." He waved and rode on.

Crosby and his men were busy castrating some yearling colts. They had one on the ground and Crosby was busy removing the seeds from his scrotum. A minimum of bleeding but the horse was in discomfort and a boy had a bucket to deposit the lost manhood in.

"Hi, Hayes. We have two more to cut, and I'll be done. Get down."

"I want to watch. I may have to do that someday."

"It isn't hard."

The men had the next colt in that harness-like rig that they pulled on from behind him. Two men on each rope, they gently laid him down. Then the crew quickly forefooted him with soft ropes. Two of them spoke and coaxed the patient talking softly to get him more relaxed. An assistant grabbed his tail, pulled it aside for the surgeon. Squatted in his near knee-high boots, Crosby used his sharp knife to make two incisions, then one at a time removed the seeds and pointed out the exact place he must separate the cord, so he wasn't proud cut and still acted like a stallion in later life.

Hayes agreed, though he had been around such cuttings before, he had let an expert do it. Crosby was one of those people. When the colt felt the surgical pain, he grunted and strained. His holders coaxed him out of it and the doctor removed the second one—same response. Then everyone stepped back, the ropes were taken off and the shaky legged animal gained his footing and walked away stiffly to join the other new geldings.

The last one to be worked was already in the rope harness they'd use to lay him gently down. The job went swiftly, and Crosby left the rest to his men, washed his hands in the bowl of water they provided, told them it was a job they did well, and he'd see them later.

Drying his hands on a flour sack towel, the two went toward the house.

"You ever do that?'

"No. I watched experts like you do it. I think I could do it all right."

"I like to cut them at about twelve months. Lots of guys run them up to two or three years old, and they've bred a mare or two, so they think from then on they're stallions."

"I have ridden some of those kinds of horses."

"Damn mess when you want to do something, and he wants to breed some horsing mare that he can't help anyway."

Hayes laughed. "Been there, done that."

"Have you heard anything about the cattle markets."

He shook his head. He'd not read a newspaper in weeks. They were full of new regulations sent in by the occupying forces. It made him so damn mad, and there was nothing he could do about it, so he quit reading about them.

"Well, we want to be on the road when the new grass breaks green. That way we will have good grazing the whole trip. The rivers will be higher at that time, but we also will have lots more water for them to drink."

"Hey, you're the man. I'm listening."

"I also want to hit a strong market. If they take all the cattle out of Texas north this spring, they might flood the market. I know not all of them who agree will go, but there will be enough anyway."

Hayes agreed with the man. The cattle driving fever was big talk anywhere he had gone the last sixty days. But not everyone could raise the money for supplies or find the drovers. It took quite an outlay to do that—banks didn't have the capital after losing all that confederate money and starting over. He never had very little of it, and his cattle sales were in Yankee dollars, so it did not affect him that much. But he felt grateful and thanked the Good Lord a lot for Crosby's efforts the year before.

They had to road brand their cattle for the brand inspection. Most road cattle had a simple bar brand on them beside the ownership one, so folks could separate one from the other—a process Crosby said not to get into.

Randy and Frank had been gathering a few more horses—just in case, and Don found him a good Mexican cook named Laredo who he promised wasn't a fireman on spicy food. Hayes settled for two Indian boys as his horse wranglers. Coyote and Burris were what they called themselves, but they could rope the needed horses very well and, in no time, had a name for every horse. Indians did well at that job, Crosby said. So, those two fit in Hayes's job.

Point riders were the most important. They set the pace of the day's drive, knew how to sweep cattle around into drinking positions that didn't drown the cattle ahead of them. Lots for him to learn and not much time for learning it all. He felt his two pals would be a big asset to his operation.

He knew Randy was like him about his wife, Carla, and maybe worse. Those two had not been married that long either. They still looked pretty moon-eyed about each other and got along. He was proud his friend had found a woman. But they faced a long separation—it would be fall getting back there to their women.

They had money to live on, and Don and his crew would protect them. They'd be much better off than most wives left behind he expected. The whole thing that gnawed at his guts was the fact he wouldn't have her right with him. And while she scoffed at having any problem, she would have the baby with him being away. Oh well, that was a price he'd pay.

Even in towns like Kerrville, they stationed a company of black soldiers with bayonets on their rifles in a tent city like situation and some Yankee talking man was the law acting like he was their row boss. Hayes avoided them all he could to save losing his temper.

Eleanor even told him she felt he'd be better off trailing cattle than being around them and losing his temper. He promised her he'd not let them arouse him, but he still felt Texans were being forced to eat lots of crow by the occupational forces who had set in to run everything.

The damn Comanche were raiding ranches all along the western edge. The rangers who had managed that situation before had been disbanded. These buffalo soldiers were all on foot and couldn't do anything about them but march out there and see the destruction and their horse tracks.

And he knew many large family ranches had given up with high debts and no markets. He had his ear to the ground too. After this drive, if successful, he'd own himself one or more of those big places. He'd told Randy and Frank his ambitions, and they agreed.

Texans ever got any money, land prices would go lots higher overnight. There was no federal land in Texas. Texas was broke, and land sales of unused rangeland would sure help the coffers. Most people got a small place to raise some food on and run some horses. Ranching was for the rich. He was part of those new ones. There would be more like him if this cattle market held up there.

"Will the Indians bother you going up there?" she'd asked him one night in bed with him.

"I don't think so, but I will find out."

"Didn't Ira say the Federals were at his store demanding to see his gun selling records?"

"He and I talked about it back when I planned to arm my crew members. He hid that business. How did they expect people to protect themselves against outlaws and warring Indians if they were unarmed?"

"Could they stop him from selling guns?"

"The U.S. Constitution says we have freedom of arms. Even in Texas they can't stop him, but they can make things difficult. They are worried about revolutions. Hell, Texans are too poor to think, let alone fight another war."

She rose up and kissed him. "That's so that my husband doesn't get in a fight with them."

He never thought a wife would be this much fun. But he'd damn sure miss her when he headed north.

One last cold spell whipped in from north Texas to finalize the month of March, but grass had broken its dormancy. Which meant it was time to head 'em and go. Activity rose. Randy rode north with Crosby's man to check out the first few stopovers.

Cattle bawled all day and night, head butting never stopped as mixed individual cattle had to decide who was higher on the social order, Cowboys were used to such fighting, but in this case, it was magnified by a thousand head—it was ear shattering when the chuck wagon and the remuda hit the road.

All the ranch hands were helping the first three days to make the quitters and fighting ones get back in the herd. Crosby promised them and the regular ranchmen could go back home in three days. By then, the cattle would know where they had to stay and for the next months the drovers would wish for a neck-by-neck charge to break the monotony of the endless drive.

When they reached the Red River crossing, the water was high and the river full of floating trees. Crosby had sent a message that he lost a young drover who had drowned crossing there. Hayes used the ferry to get the chuck wagon across. His horse wranglers swam the remuda over next without an incident. Then the blue bell lead steer went into the water and swam for the north shore. Hayes's heart was in his throat as he watched from the high point as the line of steers entered the water. Some jumped out and belly flopped, other's went into it like river otters and still more complained. A few were swept downstream. He had warned his men if they were swept downstream, and they tried to herd them in, to not to approach the north bank where there were log jams, float by them. Or they'd drown trying to get over them. Frank and two other men were already downstream on the north bank to wave the lost in to a clear shore.

Hayes's clothes, hat, and boots were in the chuck wagon when he entered the river whistling and shouting. He saw two of his naked drovers who went back into the river when they reached the far side, gave their reins to someone else and dove back in to help a comrade they thought was in trouble. The water chilled him quickly with his hand ahold of his saddle horn as his horse fought the current. A few cattle were circling downstream, but they paid no sign of quitting at his shouts for them to go on.

They'd already crossed some rivers, but this was a real challenge. Ahold of the saddle horn in his fist, he kicked to swim shivering and swallowing some fishy water. One of his men met him on the shore with a towel and his clothing.

"How are we doing?" he asked the *vaquero*.

"*Bueno. Bueno.* The *hombres* all look safe."

"Good." He sat down and pulled on his boots, checking the action in the river as he struggled to pull them on. The last drovers were in the water following the tail end of the herd.

Randy joined him and told him all were accounted for. He spoke of one *vaquero* who saved another. Hayes told him to be sure he thanked him at camp. Randy also sent some early arrivals downstream to help Frank. He estimated about a dozen steers were swept downstream, and he thought they'd get most of them back.

They rested the next day. No herds were close, and the grass was good. Hayes thanked the brave ones, and they decided they might have lost three head. The day was another extra cool one, but the men got some extra rest and were ready to ride on the next morning. He sent a letter back via the ferryman to mail to Eleanor.

To my dear wife.

Yesterday we crossed the Red River. The water was high, and we were careful.

As we move north, I wish the weather was warmer and the grass grew more.
Both act like they don't want it to be springtime. I miss you and your smiles
that always warm me. Take good care of the children and the one inside. Kiss
them for me. I won't waste a day in Kansas to get back to you.

Your husband,
Hayes.

Three Indians came to his camp that evening and asked for a steer, saying
their people were starving. He told them to come back in the morning, and
he would shoot one for them.

They thanked him, wrapped themselves in blankets, and rode some thin
horses away. He told Frank to shoot a cripple for them when the herd was
on the road. His man agreed to handle it.

All the *vaqueros* nodded, convinced the Indians looked starved and needed
the beef. Hayes felt satisfied and went to check on more details. Every day of
the drive gripped his guts more than being a company noncom under fire.
He felt he wasn't doing enough and didn't know where to start doing more.
They trekked north. His men had good control of the herd. They had not had
one stampede. He doubled his guard on those nights when thunderstorms
swept the plains.

Randy, who was riding ahead setting up their next camps, talked to him in
private one night. "Hell, Hayes, it is going good. Nothing has hurt us. I know
you want to make this a successful trip, but you can't do one thing more to
help it. Relax some. I never saw you so upset. We are two days behind Crosby
and moving along good. We will be across the Arkansas River in less than a
week, then it is less than two weeks to Abilene."

"I'll try. So much depends on us making this trip work. I have counted on
what this could do for all of us. I worry about Eleanor and how things are going
back at home. Those damn worthless occupiers will be the ruination of Texas."

"That, too, will pass."

"Randy, I hope you're right."

"The damn war is over. No one won. You told us that in Mississippi."

"I'll do better."

"You got any whiskey?" Randy asked.

"I might ought to drink a whole bottle and forget it all."

They both laughed. Hayes knew his friends were concerned. "I'll figure it out. Thanks. You and Frank are my right arms."

"We are making good progress, boss man. I'm like you. I miss my wife. I never missed anyone in the entire war. Five weeks up the trail, I miss Carla."

"Me too. Guess we've got it bad, huh?"

"Real bad."

He decided he'd do more to cheer up the crew and himself. When they crossed the Arkansas River just inside Kansas and did not lose a man or a head of stock, he went to the saloon close to the river bought several cases of bottled beer and had a man with a wagon deliver the crates to the cow camp.

They had a celebration, and many had headaches the next morning, but they went north anyway. Within a few days, he left Randy and Frank in charge and rode ahead. When he found Crosby, they rode together into Abilene.

After the Arkansas River crossing, several so-called cattle buyers dropped by talking down the Abilene market and wanting to buy their cattle to help them out before they lost their asses in Abilene.

"They just want to steal our herds," Crosby said. He shook his head at the notion they'd even tried.

Abilene looked pretty quiet when they rode down the main street. Things were going up to meet the business needs for the herds they expected. A few scantily dressed ladies of the night openly offered their services from the boardwalk to them.

Both shook their heads at them and rode on. At the Cottage House, still being built, they met Joe McCoy, the man who had made this site available. He welcomed them to Abilene.

"How was your trip?"

"Hayes and I made it fine. I lost one man in a river crossing."

"That is good news. How many cattle did you bring?"

"Each of us brought a thousand head," Hayes said.

"Good. I have buyers to bid on them. When will they be here?"

"Two days," Crosby said.

"You two will get lots of attention I guarantee you, being the first ones up here with a big herd."

They shook his hand and went back to their herds feeling much better.

Things went smoother than Hayes could believe. He soon had three bids on his cattle. The cattle cars McCoy said would be there in a few days. After much consideration he finally accepted the offer of the Illinois-based cattle brokers of Case and Sons. They agreed to pay eighty dollars apiece for every sound steer.

Hayes knew how much money that could mean for him. He about staggered coming out of the buyers offices they were using to sign the sales papers. Frank was with him that day.

"It isn't real is it?" Frank asked.

"No. It hasn't that been long ago when we were the disarmed soldiers in a Mississippi mud hole. We had nothing to look forward to that day but dragging our asses back home or wherever. And we went home the hard way. I found Eleanor and the captain's ranch he left us. No, it isn't real. He had those boys gathering wild cattle all through the war for a market he expected to open. None of us knew this would happen." He removed his hat and looked skyward.

"Frank, let's stop and thank him."

Frank swept his weathered hat off and spoke skyward. "Our most heavenly Father, we would like to thank you, sir, for the blessings you have showered upon us. Lord, we appreciate you for delivering us from those muddy fields, and back to where we belong. Thank you for helping all of us cross rivers and streams safely, and Lord protect us going home. In Jesus name we pray. Amen.

"Amen. Thanks, Frank. You are my man to handle the prayers, and I appreciate your willingness do that."

"How will we get the money home? Word will be out we've got it."

"They say Wells Fargo will move it to Texas for a fee. They will guarantee delivery or pay me."

"Where will you send it?"

"I'll send it to those bankers we saved on the road who are in Austin. I will wire them to look for it."

"Good idea. I will sleep a lot better knowing we aren't carrying it out of here."

"We better get back to work. We have lots of cattle to load in the cattle cars."

Frank agreed as they unhitched their horses, mounted, and rode for camp.

"We kinda beat the rush to get here. We're lucky. I bet that trail clear back to Texas is chock full of herds."

"Crosby sold his herd?"

"Yes, we both got the same price, but I heard lots of herds are not as uniform as ours were. People gather up anything and think they will sell them. Those farmers buying these cattle to fatten want a full-grown steer."

Fred was looking around and nodded. "They've sure got enough whores here."

"Most are anxious for customers too."

"Our *vaqueros* may check them out, huh?"

"They might. They're real good workers. Don found us some real stock drivers. He knows those people, and they know cattle. And they're horsemen. I may try to keep some of them to roundup more mavericks. Looks like we have lots more cattle drives to make."

The next days were busy. There was no rain, and the dust boiled up from all those cloven hooves. The last day loading, thunderstorms built up, and they were all drenched when the last car was slammed shut. Hayes felt relieved under the shelter of a store porch roof, and water streamed off it. He'd laid out a ten-dollar bonus to his men to go raise hell. They said they would wait to be paid their wages in Texas, so that they had money to take home. He agreed, paid them their allowance and went back to camp. He had no wish to get drunk or frolic with shady ladies himself.

The rain let up to allow him to ride back to camp, and there one of the horse wranglers took his horse. Laredo, his cook, who had become his confidant, poured him coffee and brought him a dish of apple dumplings. He thanked him.

"They are guarding your money?"

"Yes, they will take it to the bank in Austin, Texas, for me. That is how people don't get robbed going home."

"I understand, *señor*."

"Laredo, when we get home, would you go out in the brush and cook for a crew gathering mavericks?"

"I could do that. It would be less work than moving every day. Where will you do it at?"

"West of the ranch in the country where there are so many unbranded cattle. There may be lots of them rounded up now, but with a market like this one, everyone will want to catch and brand them."

"They will be like gold, huh?"

"Yes, but I want our share. Would many of these men want to do that if they were paid?"

A big smile crossed his face. "These men would love to work for you. There are no jobs in Mexico. If they could work out of a place where their families could live, they would all go to work for you. It would not take a great place either. Things you know are hard down there. Some jacals, a good well, and they would think they went to heaven."

"If I could find a place abandoned to buy, fix it up some, I could make it my headquarters for recovery of wild cattle."

"I would be glad to cook for the men or all of them. Do you know of such a place?"

"I bet I can find one."

Laredo agreed. "Like your men say about you. You will sure figure it out."

"They have lots of faith in me."

"From where you started at the end of the war, you have come a long way."

The afternoon passed quietly. Hayes even took a siesta under the chuck wagon's flap shade. He woke up when a horse came on the hard run.

"Who is it?' Hayes threw his booted foot off the cot he had been sleeping on and sat up.

"It's Frank."

Hayes slapped on his hat. His hand on the post holding up the flap, he wondered why Frank was coming in so obviously fast.

"What's wrong?"

"Some damn thugs beat up some of our men."

"Who are they?"

"I guess just some hard cases. Randy took Romero and Carl to a doctor for stitches and care."

"The others all right?"

"Yes. I made them go with Randy,"

"They went for you a horse," Laredo said.

"Good." Hayes buckled on his gun belt. "I guess we better go see how tough they are."

"Randy said, he wanted a hand in this too," Frank said, changing his saddle to a fresh horse.

"We'll get him. Where are these bad boys at?"

"Eldorado Saloon."

"Good. They won't be hard to roundup."

They left Laredo to hold the camp and raced back to town. They picked up Randy at the doc's office. His two men looked bandaged up. The other four had some black eyes and bruises, but they said they wanted to go back and help him out.

They rode their horses up the main street. Before they stopped, Hayes sent Frank around back to bar that door, so none escaped. They dismounted in front of the saloon and hitched their horses.

"Who is the leader?"

"A big hombre with a gold tooth," one of the drovers said. He pointed to a tooth next to his eyetooth.

When Hayes led the ranch crew into the saloon, a big guy stood up over a chair in the back. "I told you gawdamn Mexicans to get the hell out of here."

Randy told the bartender to put his hands on the bar and held his gun in his fist. The man rested them on the bar.

"You the leader of them damn Mex's?" the big one demanded.

"I am. They work for me. They drove a thousand head of cattle up here and have money to buy their drinks."

"By God, I'll clean house with you cowboy." He charged Hayes.

Hayes grabbed up a captain's chair swung it in a circle that busted him in the face. He went to his knees as the legs flew off the chair. Hayes drew what was left over his head, and the thick seat struck the back of his skull, and he went face down with a great groan.

The remains of the chair tossed aside with his fist again around the hickory handle of his pistol he slashed him in the mouth rising up. Hayes felt the man's teeth give under it. The man spit three teeth out in a bloody mass. Hayes's boot toe struck him in the shoulder and turned him over on his back.

"I'm taking that gold one for the boy to have a trophy for your beating him up and him half your size. He works at the XYZ Ranch if you ever need to find him that's near Kerrville, Texas."

He swept it up and shoved the tooth in his pocket.

"I guess now my Mexican men can drink in here." He searched around the room for any sign of a threat. Pour us all a round of beer," he told the bartender who obeyed him.

"Where did you come from, mister?" a bystander asked.

"Kerrville, Texas. West of San Antonio."

"You always use chairs like that to fight with?"

"I'll use anything it takes to win. I needed an evener for him."

A man with a silver badge on his vest came charging through the bat wing doors. "What's happening in here?"

His elbows on the bar and his back to it, Hayes indicated the big man lying on his back moaning. "He fell over his own boots and broke out some teeth on the chair he ran into. Let me buy you a beer, marshal. I'm buying everyone else's."

"I could use a beer, sir."

"Bartender, bring the marshal a beer while he figures out how this man broke the peace and tranquil friendliness of this saloon and needs to serve a few days in the calaboose."

His crew laughed quietly. Others were amused.

The marshal drank his beer. Then he thanked Hayes and told some of the onlookers to grab the big boy's feet and arms to haul him to jail where Doc could examine his injuries as well.

Hayes thanked the lawman when they carried the groggy bully out the batwing doors. Then he gathered his crew, and they headed back to camp.

Frank asked him riding home if he had dreaded facing that big guy.

"I knew I had to stop him. And my fists would only get me inside his long reach, and he'd beat me up. So, I used the chair to stop him. Those legs were stout, stouter than I thought before they broke and stopped him. Then the back portion was still okay, and the seat looked thick enough to slam his head hard. To bust his teeth out would require metal, so I used the gun barrel. They came out easier than most. Ricky, you still got your gold tooth?"

The younger of the two-bandaged drovers said, "Oh, *si*. I will wear it all my life on a chain. I wish I could have seen the fight you had with him."

"Naw. It didn't last long. It was over fast."

"Boy, Hayes, he was like a steam engine piston hitting me."

"I knew that when I saw you at the doctor. He made me mad there. You boys weren't hurting anyone in that bar. Let's start home tomorrow. We can drink *cerveza* at home."

They cheered.

After supper, Laredo said to him, "Those boys are all ready to roundup cattle for you when they get home if they can have a week off to go home and come back. I told him about your plans. They think you are one tough hombre. How big was he?"

"Big as a grizzly bear."

They packed up and started back south. They faced a real tough storm the third night, but didn't get blown away. The rain did them some good cooling the temperature for a few days. The killdeer chased bugs their horses stirred up, and meadowlarks sang. Without the cattle, they made good time skirting herd after herd after herd, his outfit making twenty to thirty miles in a day. He bought some grain for the mules, to keep them going, but exchanging horses, they didn't need any.

"You know most outfits sell their horses and wagons when they get up there," Randy told him. "I have talked to several, and that was their plans."

"Why do that? I know we will start back gathering cattle and next spring come right back up here. That wagon of ours is sturdy. We will need the remuda to catch cattle when we get home. Be foolish to sell it up there and turn around and have to buy another one."

"Most of them boys with those other herds tell me that they won't get paid to ride back."

"Frank, these boys are our permanent employees. I'm not treating them like that."

"I ain't forgot coming home from Mississippi with no money. I sure like this a helluva lot better."

"How many we taking up the trail next year?"

"Six thousand."

"Really?" Frank asked.

"You'll have one herd. Randy one and me one. Can we do it?"

Frank shook his head in disbelief. "We'll have to hire lots more help to just brand them."

"I intend to start hiring them the day we get home."

"Hell, you know I'll go along with whatever you need. You and Randy have wives—"

"Want us to find you one?" Hayes asked him.

"Sounds kinda silly, me asking that of you, but help me."

"You need to learn how to dance. Eleanor and Juanita can teach you how. The rest will come."

"Aw, hell, I get rubber knees around pretty women, and my tongue gets too thick to say anything."

"Anyone can do as much ramrodding as you do for me, can learn to dance and talk to women."

"I'd be grateful if you would help me."

"No bitching when you find and marry her. Don't tell me she nags you all the time, and I will help find you one."

They both laughed and rode on. Frank was a tough guy, but like he told Hayes, he went to mush around a woman that he wanted to impress. He only needed some starch in his backbone, and he'd be all right.

Where would he start his expanded ranching at next? Lots to do and figure and the word would be out about the Abilene market. They might not be the first ones there next year. Maybe his mouth was bigger than his brain about doing all that—no, he intended to do it. He might not ever be the biggest thing in Texas, but he aimed to get on the top step with them guys.

He simply needed to get after it.

———————

WHEN HAYES REINED IN THE hot sweaty horse and spotted his wife's red hair coming out the front door with a bundle—he knew she carried his first child in her arms.

Out of breath, at last on the porch, he kissed her and took the baby.

"It's a boy. Hayes Jon McBroom the second."

"A fine baby. How are you?' he asked with the child in his arms.

"He cries a lot," Rachel said.

"Is he sad?" he asked his daughter.

She pulled him down to tell him. "No, he just wants more titty."

He had to contain his amusement. "I see."

His wife must have heard it and shook her head in disapproval.

With a grin he shook his head. "She's only telling the truth."

"You must've hurried to get here?"

"I did. To get to see you and the children." He hefted his daughter in his arms. "And I am home."

His wife shook her head. "Good to have you home. I have missed you."

"Me too." He followed her into the house.

"I got your letter. I guessed from that it was a big success."

"Yes, unbelievable. And I plan to go back next year with more."

She shook her head putting the baby in the cradle. "I'll fix you some food. I bet you haven't eaten."

"I'd rather hold you," he said putting the girl down.

"I know, but first things first. I bet Don and Lupe will be here shortly. They have been waiting for you too."

"Everything is all right?"

"Oh, sure, but you are the boss and have been gone."

He agreed and knelt down to talk to the boy. "You all right, big man?"

"I'm fine."

"Are you getting to ride?"

He shook his head.

"My wranglers get here. They will show you how to ride a horse."

He smiled.

"They are great helpers."

She poured him some coffee, looked up, and told the foreman and his wife to come in.

Hayes hugged her and shook his hand, then indicated the kitchen table and chairs.

"You look thinner," Don said.

"I am fine. Aside from a fight in a saloon with a bully who had beat up two of our men, we had little trouble. Those *vaqueros* are wonderful help. One or two need to learn how to swim better, but they did a wonderful job. They're going to be part of the ranch force helping us round up more unbranded cattle. Laredo has agreed to stay and feed them. He is also a good employee. I thank you for hiring them."

"Good. We make progress. There are some people jealous of your cattle drive saying you stole some of their cattle to drive them north."

"I told the law that the brand inspector passed on them and nothing they could do. He agreed."

"Who are they?"

"Norton Bales and his boys."

Things settled down a lot in a few days. His foreman, Don, hired twenty more *vaqueros* to work on branding wild cattle. Randy headed up that operation. Good thing that he brought the horses and chuck wagon back. He needed both of them and his cook, Laredo. Best of all he was back with his wife and the children. A situation he never dreamed about in all his wishing to find a place. Here it was mid-day, kid's to care for, his foreman anxious to hear about his success, and all he could think about were his plans to make love to his wife.

TWO WEEKS LATER, HE AND Frank were in a small settlement called Two Creek about two days ride from home, looking in that area for wild cattle and perhaps even a ranch set up to buy. Hayes had conversed with the bartender, Michael, some in the El Reno saloon. He was an older man, about bald, who had seen some tough deals in his life and had a good hold on things. Hayes figured running a saloon on the far edge of the law wasn't ever easy.

"You ever hear of the Spanish Grant given to the Oliver family?" the saloon owner asked.

Hayes shook his head.

"It's a lot like Captain King's deal was when he found it. The king of Spain gave families big holdings in the new world and expected them to populate these places with farmers and make settlements to pay taxes back to him."

Hayes nodded. "I heard about it but not that one. Oliver Grant?"

"Oliver, that was the family name."

"Where is it?"

"West of here. They tried settling it several times, but Comanche and Mexican bandits raided it. So, they gave up, and it's been empty for years. Even ghost stories are told about it."

Hayes could hardly believe the man's story. "No one has it now?"

"I think some hard cases use it for a hideout now."

"Who is that?"

"Braxton is the guy that heads them. Cory Braxton is wanted but no one wants to face his wrath. He's tough, mean, and has escaped many jails and lawmen."

"In other words, this is a bulldog that bites?"

"You're damn right. I keep two sawed off shotguns under the bar loaded for when they come in here."

"Me and Frank may need to go look at that place. Draw me a map. Tomorrow we'll go see about this guy and if I am even interested in it."

"So, you will go prepared is all. I want to warn you."

"We will be when we go. Draw the map."

"This is Two Creek, and you go west to Silver Springs. It's only a watering hole. Turn northwest there, and you can find the old road they used to come up from Mexico on with ox carts, huh?"

"Yeah. Are there any buildings left?"

"I think so. They say the old house needs work, but it once was a castle. Just be careful. You look like a hard man, but everyone in his gang is a hard case."

Hayes downed the last of his beer, paid the man well for his information, and told Frank they better go see about it in the morning. His one-eyed buddy agreed, and they left the saloon.

Outside in the sparkling midday heat, he smiled over at Frank while tightening his cinch. "We may have found heaven."

Frank chuckled. "Or the fires of hell."

"Maybe tha,t too. Let's ride, daylight's burning up."

They camped at Silver Springs that evening, and Hayes could see the long ago made cart ruts going north like the man spoke about. At one time, it might have been a highway even. Texas independence had cut off the Mexican traffic years earlier. Many noble families went south of the border rather than live under the rule of the rough as a cob Texans who had won and stole their land and traditions from them.

They picketed their two packhorses out of sight and hobbled them. The next morning, they rode northwest on the road, being careful not to be exposed should anyone come down the road. No one came, and they soon found themselves in some oak and cedar clad hills. At last, about to ride up on it, they discovered a large valley, and in his field glasses, he could see the faded red tile on the roof of the two-story house. Campfire smoke hung close to the ground. Several women and naked brown children moved about. Their shrill voices carried on the rising wind.

In the lens, they saw not one man, but there was no telling. Where there were women, men came around or back to them sometime. No horses in the corrals meant to Hayes that they were off on a raid or some activity. He doubted it was rounding up cattle. He'd seen enough—lots of cloven tracks and cow pies both new and old on his way into there to know this region was loaded with cattle. No doubt unmarked ones too.

Where was the chief outlaw at? His name was Cory Baxter. A name he'd never heard about but that meant nothing. In his three years in the war, he'd lost track of many men while fighting in a foreign land called Mississippi.

An hour later, they were on foot and closer to the activity. The men were still not visible. Both he and Frank carried rifles, and when Hayes was satisfied there were no men there, they both made themselves known to the working women in camp.

"Where are the men?"

A tall woman maybe thirty, tossed her black hair back and never answered his question. "Who in the hell are you?"

"The guy looking for answers. Where are they?"

"Who knows? Are you Rangers?"

"There ain't no Rangers anymore."

"Good. One raped me once."

"I doubt that. He may have said he was one. Rangers never raped women I ever heard about."

"Mister you were never a teenage Hispanic girl either."

"My apology then. When do you expect him to come back?"

"How should I know?"

"I figure you run this camp when he is away, right?"

She nodded. Her dark eyes were hard set. "Sometimes."

The other women laughed uneasy like at her words.

"You bounty hunters?"

He shook his head. "We're ranchers looking for a place."

"Not this one. This is his place."

Hayes made a pained face at her answer. "He don't own it."

"He is a big man. He owns it by his fists and guns."

"That ain't good enough in Texas."

She laughed out loud and scoffed at him. "You aren't tough enough to take it from him."

"Lady, I am here aren't I?" He dismounted. "Get everyone around here. Sit in a circle, and we will wait for them to return."

"They won't be back today."

"You said you don't know. I have many days to wait. Get them and the children out here. We start in a circle today. The cottonwoods will shade you and the wind cool us."

Frank checked out every building and place they could hide and soon had the rest rounded up. He found some wine and brought a half-filled case of dust floured corked bottles.

"Can they have it?" he asked Hayes.

"What's your name?" he asked the woman in charge.

"Carissa."

"Get an opener and some cups. You may as well enjoy the rest of the day and the wine."

The women toasted the two and laughing passed the open wine bottles around. The occasion soon became an all-girl party. One asked permission to go get a couple of guitars. Hayes agreed but warned her, "No tricks."

They soon were singing the songs of Mexico. The wild horse, the lover that left, and Camellia. Hayes left Frank in charge and went about seeing they had few possessions or wealth. There was half a steer carcass under a wet canvas shroud hanging in an empty shed, blocked off from dogs and other animals. The wet cover kept it cool enough to eat for many days. No great riches in sight, but it might be what he needed for his second place.

The women kept drinking the wine and some got up and danced with castanets. The clicking in their graceful hands set the beat and away they went shifting their hips. Some even became bare to the waist and showed off. Others cheered them on. This freedom and the alcohol really made them free spirits. While they were having fun acting tempting, Hayes knew it really bothered Frank.

"Dance with one of them," he said.

Frank did, and they took turns dancing with him. Mexicans can dance in the dust. These women were no exception. Still no outlaws returned. If they left the place, then the outlaws would know his purpose and become fortified. So, all they could do was wait. He sent Frank to get their packhorses the next morning. He returned in a few hours, and they unsaddled them and shared some Arbuckle coffee with the women now free to do what they had to do.

He told Carissa he wanted none of them or any children hurt and for them to seek shelter in case a fight broke out.

She scoffed at him and said that Baxter would kill him and Frank in a snap of her fingers.

"You can believe what you want lady. But me and that one-eyed buddy of mine have killed more men than you can count."

She went off shaking her head high. "Not Baxter."

"We will see," Hayes said after her.

Midday he spotted their dust first in the distance, then heard the horses coming and made all the women and children get inside a small adobe house and closed the door. Then he and Frank took up defensive positions with their rifles. He saw the headman spur his lathered horse and gallop for the house when he was a hundred feet away. Hayes fired a shot in the dust. That forced the man to rein up.

"Don't go for that gun!" Hayes warned him.

But to no avail, Baxter slapped the Colt in his holster out and Hayes put a bullet in his chest, the man's arm dropped, his gun fired in the dust, and the horse pitched him off.

Carissa screamed.

"Stay back. He's dead," Hayes told her.

The rest of the men reined up their horses and looked at them in disbelief.

"Throw down your guns or die. We have you covered."

Obviously in shock over their famous leader's demise in the dust at that moment under the body of his crying woman, begging for him to live, they obeyed, dropped their weapons and came on in. Dismounted, the two checked them for more weapons, then made them sit on the ground.

Hayes picked out a boy among them and sent him to catch the outlaw's horse which was standing ground tied off in the low brush. Dutifully he returned the horse to them.

Hayes called for one of the women to get a blanket. Carissa had stood up with his blood on the front of her dress. "What will you do to him?"

"He has a bounty on his head. I will collect it."

"Where will he be buried?"

"The law will do that. I have no idea."

She glared at him. "You are one cold blooded bastard."

"No, he made the choice to give up or be killed. He chose death. Now wrap him up and load him on his horse," he said to two of the men.

They obeyed.

"Come here," Frank said to Hayes from checking his saddlebags.

Hayes soon discovered there was lots of money in both sides. No doubt the loot of his crimes. He took a small cotton sack of money out and called to a woman in the group he knew could handle it.

"Antonia, come here."

She came holding her skirts out of the dust.

"This money will get all of you back to Mexico. I know you will need your men to help get all of you home, so I will not arrest them. But make them take you home. In Texas, they will still look for them if they ever come back, and they will hang them all, too."

"*Si, señor.*" She curtsied for him and took the money.

Frank oversaw them loading and tying Baxter's body down over his saddle. Satisfied, he took the reins. The men were marched down to the corral, and Frank guarded them seated on the ground while Hayes loaded the packs on their horses.

Then Hayes called the woman he had paid the money to and gave her all the supplies they had in the panniers for them to eat. The other women thanked him too. He shoved his rifle in the scabbard and mounted his horse. Frank did the same, leading Baxter's pony.

The women had the panniers emptied of the food he gave them, and Antonia led the two up to Hayes. "*Muchas gracias.*"

He nodded. Still lots to do, but he hoped that his wife loved her new ranchero. He was already taking a liking to it. They headed for the home place and some law to accept the outlaw's body. He'd need a good lawyer to wing this deal—but he had enough money in those saddlebags not to touch his own wealth to do it.

After three more bitter years of occupation, Texas stopped eating crow, and the troops left. And the Texas Rangers returned to end the lawlessness and Indian raids.

DUSTY RICHARDS GREW UP RIDING horses and watching his western heroes on the big screen. He even wrote book reports for his classmates, making up westerns since English teachers didn't read that kind of book. His mother didn't want him to be a cowboy, so he went to college, then worked for Tyson Foods and auctioned cattle when he wasn't an anchor on television.

His lifelong dream, though, was to write the novels he loved. He sat on the stoop of Zane Grey's cabin and promised he'd one day get published, as well. In 1992, that promise became a reality when his first book, *Noble's Way*, hit the shelves. In the years since, he's published over 160 more, winning nearly every major award for western literature along the way. His 150th novel, *The Mustanger and the Lady*, was adapted for the silver screen and released as the motion picture *Painted Woman* in 2017. In a review for the movie, *True West* magazine proclaimed Dusty "the greatest living western fiction writer alive."

Sadly, Dusty passed away in early 2018, leaving behind a legion of fans and a legacy of great western writing that will live on for generations.

www.ingramcontent.com/pod-product-compliance
Lightning Source LLC
Chambersburg PA
CBHW032046240626
47154CB00003B/1096